# TIME AND TIDE

# Mike Simmons

Enquiries concerning reproduction outside those terms should be sent to the publishers
Paper Girders Publishing
07932907653
Email papergirders@gmail.com
www.papergirderspublishing.com

**Proof reading and editing by Fran Thorne**

**ISBN 9798430795498**

British Library Cataloguing in Publication Data
A catalogue record for this book is available from the British Library

Dedicated to Alan Padwick
20th June 1940 - 24th January 2022

The Talented illustrator of my books

# Contents

# CHAPTER ONE

## Receding Water

There was a bleak eeriness to Muckle Farm, a bygone ghostly shell which had never been laid to rest. The wind from the surrounding fallow fields howled and rattled the corrugated roofs of the old barn and milking sheds. In the dusty yard, rusting pieces of farm machinery sat like deserted props in a darkened theatre. The wooden beams and roof of the farm cottage creaked and groaned with old age. Grimy cracked windows stemmed the sun from entering, leaving a constant chill clinging to the dank air. At the yard entrance, the metal gate swung wildly, holding onto the post by one broken hinge.

Generations of the Pearson family had farmed here at the side of the canal since 1865, but mad cow disease in 1986 had wiped out the dairy herd and the farm, already struggling financially, was put up for sale. There never was a buyer and eventually the present owners, Owen Pearson and his family, abandoned the farm and moved away.

Rocket Ron checked the padlock on the front door of the cottage, one of many he had replaced. He was the self-appointed guardian of Muckle Farm. The local waifs and strays had been known to break in and use it as a squat, and worse. Ron's narrowboat was moored a short distance away. He had lived in this area since the seventies and knew the Pearsons well. His two pet ferrets, Frankie and Freddie, chased each other in and out of the empty barn.

He checked his watch. It was eight o'clock. The setting sun was casting long finger shadows across the old buildings. As dusk fell it always reminded him of the story of Daisy Kearns, a twenty four year old Land Army girl, who in 1943 had gone missing from the farm. Despite a police investigation, albeit scaled back due to the war effort, and an intense search of the surrounding area, she was never found, alive or dead.

A lone crow, perched on a fence post. watched him and the two ferrets leave. It was always there, its small brown eyes darting to and fro. Ron was never quite sure if it was the same one each time.

'See you tomorrow,' he called, as he passed the shiny black bird.

There were two boats moored alongside the towpath, his and his friend Rose's. Before the heavy rains at Easter he had been moored further away, but after the landslip which had nearly engulfed her boat, he had decided to moor closer to her. Rose, a gentle, slightly eccentric soul lived alone with only her cat and stuffed bears to keep her company. Each bear, once loved and now abandoned, had been left by her boat, some in an awful state of neglect. She would carefully clean, repair and name them before placing them in the trunk with the others.

It had taken four weeks for the flood waters at Kirtby and elsewhere to slowly subside. Tim, Zed and Dwain stood alongside Thor and Odin below Kirtby Lock. This weekend was their first opportunity to take the two boats back to their mooring in Tiddledurn since having to abandon them at Easter due to the flood waters.

Odin and Thor, the butty without an engine, were converted working boats. In their heyday they had transported cargo to and from the London docks. Now fitted with canvas roofs and bunk beds they carried youth groups on trips.

Tim, who had been born and bred on the waterways and owned the boats, looked around him. He shook his head. 'What a mess.'

The two boys, Zed and Dwain agreed. A thick layer of sludgy silt covered the towpath and grass at the edge of the canal. Tall reed banks had been flattened by the weight of the water and an overturned dinghy bobbed about, still tied to a rickety garden landing stage.

Tim turned the ignition key on Odin. Without hesitation the engine burst into life. He patted the roof. 'That's my boy.' He did not subscribe to boats being called 'she'; after all, unlike ships of old, narrowboats never had a female figurehead. Before leaving the mooring, Zed and Dwain rolled back the canvas roof on each boat to let fresh air circulate around the damp smelling interiors.

Keeping both boats lashed alongside each other they were able to cruise the short distance to Kirtby Basin where they could turn. A pile of discarded, soggy sandbags stood in front of the small shops and houses which fronted the basin. A green wheelie bin floated past the stern, its lid flapping open and closed like a fish deprived of water. Disorientated moorhens zig zagged across the canal with chicks who had survived the flood, paddling franticly to keep up with their parents. Great clumps of river weed wrenched from their roots floated as green patchwork on the muddy brown surface.

As Tim throttled the two seventy foot boats around, Raymond, the overweight, florid faced waterways man, called to him from the bank.
'Keep an eye on your prop, there's a lot of debris under the water.'

Tim waved. 'Cheer's mate, and thanks for watching the boats. I owe you a pint.'

Raymond laughed 'I'll keep you to that, you tight old devil.'

Having cleared Kirtby Locks on the return journey Tim and the boys dropped Thor astern of Odin in the towing position. The bridge holes were too narrow to go through when breasted alongside each other. Zed steered Thor, while Dwain stood beside him listening to music on his headphones. Zed nudged him.

The arable fields either side of the canal showed the effects of the heavy rains. Most had lost whatever crops were planted there. Others still resembled wide boating lakes. Tim waved urgently to signal that he was slowing down as a part submerged waterlogged tree was blocking their way. As Thor did not have an engine it was impossible for Zed to suddenly reduce momentum, so as the towline between the two boats slackened, he steered to the port side to avoid hitting Odin. Dwain stopped jigging about to his Hip Hop and took off his headphones.

'What's 'appening dude?'

'Dunno,' replied Zed. 'I think there's something in the water.'
Dwain chuckled. 'Maybe it's a bloated body, drowned in the floods.'

Zed shook his head. 'You're sick man.'
Dwain laughed and carried on listening to his music.

Carefully Tim nudged the wallowing tree towards the bank. Then taking out his phone he rang Raymond to inform him of the obstacle so it could be removed or secured. Giving an onward wave to Zed he pushed down on Odin's throttle. There was a sudden jolt as the towline tightened. It was only a short distance now to Melbury Lock. Once through there and the boats would be back home at Tiddledurn again, where Tim lived with his partner Peggy.

Ben pulled his van over at the side of the road. He had driven the short distance from his boat moored on the canal to an area between the village of Tiddledurn and Melbury town. He checked the address from the note which his partner Remi had given him that morning. The little black and white chequered flag on the sat nav indicated that he had arrived at his destination. Turning off the engine he stepped out.  There was no sight of a property in the tree lined road, just a pair of tall, black, iron gates, partly concealed by overgrown bushes. Either side stood two square brick posts, each with a hideous looking stone creature on top. He checked for a bell or intercom; there was none. Peering through the bars of the gate he could see a gravel driveway cutting through lush rhododendrons. A Royal Mail van slowed and stopped beside him.

'You alright mate?' asked the postman.
Ben showed him the piece of paper with the address on.

'Yeah, that's here,' he replied. 'Just open the gates and go in.'

'Cheer's mate,' called Ben.

Cautiously he walked part way along the drive. Reaching the muddy pond choked by water lilies, he froze as two very vocal black Labradors came charging towards him. There was a shrill whistle from beyond the bushes and the two dogs suddenly changed course. Moments later a woman in a battered Barbour jacket and green wellies appeared with the two dogs beside her.

'Now Milo, Morgan, go and say hello nicely to the young man.'

Ben patted their heads. 'They're all bark,' she said, holding out her hand for him to shake. 'You must be Ben, the carpenter. My husband told me you were coming to give us an estimate.' She looked around her. 'Don't you have a vehicle?'

Ben nodded. 'I do, but I didn't like to just drive in.'

She gave a husky smoker's laugh. 'Oh, don't worry about that. The days of the tradesman's entrance are long gone. You go and get it and I'll put the kettle on.'

From the moment he drove into the open courtyard it was obvious that Hartly Manor, family seat of the Barrington Gores since the sixteenth century, was a shadow of its former self. The breeze ruffled the invading ivy which clung to the exterior walls. Still an imposing aristocratic pile it clearly required urgent investment.

Lady Barrington Gore stood waiting by the solid oak front door.

'Do come in young man. Tea's made.' Milo and Morgan sat beside her, tails wagging enthusiastically.

Ben stepped into an expansive circular entrance hall with black and white chequered flooring. It reminded him of the symbol on his sat nav. A gallery of heavy framed pictures adorned the walls, most were of stern looking men, some in military uniform.

'They're my husband's ancestors,' she explained.

Ben nodded. 'That's nice.'

She chuckled. 'I am afraid some of them were not that nice at all. This way.'

They crossed the hall, passing a sweeping staircase with heavily polished bannisters. The drawing room was not of this century. Ben admired the dark, solid oak furniture and expensive rugs, albeit frayed around the edges. Nothing IKEA here, he thought. Lady Barrington Gore ushered him towards a coffee table set in front of a wide bay window. Richly coloured drapes faded by time and the sun hung to floor length from a stout wooden pole.

He half expected her to ring a bell and the butler would appear with the tea, but no, it was already laid out on a wicker tray. To his surprise there were no bone china cups, just two ordinary looking blue mugs. Milo and Morgan sat drooling in anticipation of a treat.

'My husband tells me you live on a narrowboat?' she asked, pouring the tea.

Ben nodded. 'That's right. My partner Remi and I escaped the rat race and moved down here.'

'That must be terribly exciting, a real adventure,' she said, offering him a biscuit.

'Yeah, we like it,' he replied. 'You meet a lot of interesting people.'

She threw the dogs a biscuit each. 'My son and daughter went on a narrowboat with the school; they loved it.'

'Are they at a boarding school?' asked Ben.

Again, she gave a loud, husky laugh. 'Good grief no, we couldn't afford that. George and Phoebe go to Melbury Academy.'

Ben nibbled the edges of the chocolate digestive biscuit. At home on the boat he would have consumed it in two bites, but felt it impolite to do that here.

'So, what is it you want me to do?' he asked her.

'We have a cellar,' she said. That did not surprise him. 'It's where the wine used to be kept but now we use it for storage.'

Ben nibbled some more of his biscuit, resisting the urge to stuff it all in his mouth.

She continued. 'The other day my husband put his foot through one of the steps. I fear the whole thing is rotten.'

'Must be pretty old,' he replied.

She smiled. 'Yes, like everything else here.'

After finishing their tea, she stood up. 'Would you like to see it?'

She waited by the door to the cellar whilst Ben inspected the dimly lit staircase. As he emerged the grandfather clock in the hall struck twelve.

'What do you think?' she asked.

'I should be able to do that,' he replied, brushing the dust from his fleece. 'In the meantime, I wouldn't go down there unless you really must, it's riddled with woodworm. I'll do you a quote and drop it round tomorrow if that's ok.'

She thanked him for coming and waved as he walked across the courtyard towards his van. He took out his phone and texted Smokey Joe. 'Guess who's working for the upper classes?'
Milo and Morgan chased him down the drive.

# CHAPTER TWO

## New School

As usual Betty, Zed's gran, had gone to bed late and risen early to try and avoid the intrusive dreams which came with the darkness. Drawing back the curtains, she looked out from the window of the small flat above the butcher's shop in Tiddledurn. Beyond St Mark's church with the tall spire opposite she could see the village green with its duck pond, children's playground and thatched cottages around the perimeter. An occasional car or agricultural vehicle passed along the narrow High Street below.

This tranquil scene was a world away from her flat on the eighth floor of a tower block on Rotherhithe Road in South London. There, the traffic was relentless, even in the middle of the night, as was the sound of planes skimming overhead as they prepared to land at London City Airport. A brief walk to the local shops from the estate would leave her eyes watering from the exhaust fumes spewed out from passing buses and lorries, then invariably the lift in the tower block would not be working, which meant a long haul carrying the shopping up the stairs. But for all that she missed the hustle and bustle of the big city. Born into a family of London dockers it was all she had ever known. Now the consequences and legacy of her daughter Amanda's passing meant she and Zed would never again be able to safely return to that estate, nor would his friend Dwain who had become unwittingly caught up in the fallout.

She blinked back a tear as she considered the upheaval and enormity of it all. At her time of life, she could have done without it.

'Oh Amanda, Amanda,' she said softly. 'How could you do this to us?'

Mr. Strout, the butcher dressed in his striped apron and flat cap, waved to her as he loaded some meat into his van. She waved back. He always made her laugh with his flirtatious ways and naughty jokes. It was nice to be called 'a young lady again'. On the sideboard was a picture of her grandson, Zed, in his school uniform. His cheeky grin made her smile as she picked it up. 'At least I still have you, my love,' she said, blowing dust from the glass.

It was one of the few possessions she now had left. All the furniture in the flat belonged to her friend Peggy who had lived here previously after losing her live-aboard narrowboat, Turtle One, to a fire from which she had been lucky to escape. Ironically, it was the destructive nature of this element that had now caused Betty to seek sanctuary in Tiddledurn. The difference being that Peggy's was a tragic accident, whereas the blaze at Betty's home in London was a deliberate attempt by people to intimidate and destroy.

Of course, she missed Zed not living with her, as he had done since being born to his mother Amanda, Betty's daughter. But it was only a one-bedroom flat and, now a teenager, he was happier staying with his friend Dwain on Peggy's new narrowboat, Turtle Two. The school bus which took Zed and Dwain to Melbury Academy stopped just along the street, so at least she saw them in the mornings and after school when it dropped them off.

The bedside alarm on Turtle Two went off at six thirty, followed minutes later by a phone call from Tim to make sure the shrill beeping had not been ignored. Mondays came round far too quickly for Zed and Dwain. On Saturday they had helped Tim bring the two boats, Odin and Thor, back from Kirtby Locks to Tiddledurn. On Sunday morning they had gone for a paddle along the canal in Blackjack, their double seated canoe. The afternoon had been spent doing homework.

Zed and Dwain groaned then reluctantly rolled out of their sleeping bags, showered, and changed into their new school uniforms. Melbury Academy's attire was more formal than they had worn at the comprehensive school in Rotherhithe. Maroon blazer, grey trousers, white shirt, and blue and gold ties. How they hated wearing ties. Leaving the narrowboat which was moored astern of Tim's community boats, Odin and Thor, they wandered the short distance along the towpath towards Tim's cottage by the lock. Little was said between them as they were both still half asleep.

Peggy was waiting with their breakfast. Tim, who was on his third brew of the morning, laughed as they came through the front door. 'Blimey, it's the walking dead.'

He got no response. Ready on the table were corn flakes, fresh orange juice and toast.

'What time did you two get to sleep last night?' asked Peggy.

Zed muttered something in audible.

'I take it that means late?' said Tim.

Peggy sat down at the table. 'If you can't be trusted to go to bed early on school nights then we'll have to take the television away.'

Tim chuckled. 'It's not the television, it's those blasted phones.'

Peggy nodded. 'Then you will have to leave them here before you go to the boat.'

The boys looked horrified. 'It's up to you,' said Tim. 'You're not getting enough rest.'

After leaving the cottage the boys walked across the village green towards the High Street. Before boarding the bus to Melbury Academy, they would call in to see Betty at the flat.

She was waiting with their packed lunches which she provided for them each day.

'You two look tired,' she said.

Zed yawned. 'We're ok, Gran.'

Dwain slumped onto the sofa. 'I hate Mondays.'

Gran said. 'That was a song by the Boom Town Rats.'

The boys glanced at each other. 'Never heard of 'em,' said Zed.

She laughed. 'Well, I doubt you have, it was in the Seventies!'

Dwain checked the time on his phone. 'We need to go.'

They both gave her a kiss. 'Have a nice day, Gran,' said Zed.

'I will,' she replied, 'I'm meeting Peggy for lunch.'

A group of maroon blazered youngsters gathered outside the newsagents where the school bus would stop. Some were interacting with each other though most were either texting or checking their likes on facebook.

Dwain had noticed her before; the tall, slim girl with long brown hair that kissed her shoulders. She was standing next to a boy slightly shorter but with the same strong, clear, bone features. He guessed it was her brother. Zed and Dwain had been at Melbury Academy now for four weeks. Dwain, the more gregarious of the two, had little trouble forging friendships. Zed, shy to the point of seeming dismissive, hung back.

The school bus, which was actually a fifty-two-seater luxury coach, glided to a stop. The automatic doors folded back and the students filed on board. It was always the same driver who always said the same thing. 'Morning guys, all aboard the Melbury Express.' Dwain thought there was something weird about a middle-aged man calling people 'guys.' Anyway, nobody took any notice of him as they fell into the seats and plugged their earphones in.

The girl with the long brown hair sat right at the back of the coach with three other girls. Every so often Dwain could hear them giggling loudly.

'This beats walking to school in London,' Zed said, as he closed his eyes and relaxed his body into the comfortable seats. Dwain nudged him. 'Don't fall asleep man, we'll be there soon.'
He opened his eyes. 'I'm not, I was just thinking.'
'About what?' asked Dwain.
Zed shrugged. 'Just things.'

Melbury Academy, formally a comprehensive, was situated just on the outskirts of the town. Amongst other things it prided itself on its sporting achievements and had open field spaces and facilities that London state schools could only dream of. This suited Dwain who excelled at all sporting disciplines. Zed on the other hand could take it or leave it, preferring football if pushed.

Mrs Gerta Holmesbran, a small but formidable lady of German origin, was the head of Year eleven and known throughout the school as 'The Dragon Lady'. She had been made aware by the Head Teacher of the reason why Zed and Dwain had to leave London and change schools. She kept a close eye on them, particularly Dwain who was one of only three mixed race pupils at the school of twelve hundred students. It was important to her that they settled into their new routine without any problems, and woe betide anybody who created any for them.

After the two boys had finished their breakfast and left for school, Peggy and Tim walked along to where Odin and Thor were moored by the old stables. Tim pushed a wheelbarrow loaded with the equipment he and Peggy would need. Having sat idle for four weeks at Kirtby Locks both boats were in much need of some urgent, tender loving care. The local pigeons and sea gulls had been in competition to create as much mess as possible on the canvas roofs. The interior smelt damp and musty, everything needed a good clean and airing. Peggy filled all the pots and pans with water and put them on the stove to boil.

She checked her watch; she had four hours before meeting Betty for lunch in Tiddledurn. Tim connected the high-pressure hose to a portable generator and set about blasting the bird droppings from the fabric roofs. Peggy had used some of the hot water to make tea. She called Tim inside the boat.

'Wretched flying vermin,' he mumbled to himself, coming down the steps. They sat down at one of the folding trestle tables and Tim took a mouthful of tea, nice and strong as he liked it. 'Did Zed say who that letter was from the other day?'

Peggy shook her head. 'No, and I never asked.'

Tim thought for a moment. 'It's a bit odd though, don't you think? And how did they get the address?'

Peggy shrugged. 'I don't know. Maybe it's from a friend in London.'

He laughed. 'Get with it Peg, youngsters don't send each other letters these days, if they ever did. It's all texting, and anyway, I don't think he had any friends up there apart from Dwain.'

'Well, it was obviously private,' she replied, 'as he didn't seem too keen on revealing the sender.'

'Exactly,' said Tim. 'It's weird. I mean he's normally so open about things.'

There was a knock on the roof and Rocket Ron appeared at the hatch. Frankie and Freddie, his two ferrets, tumbled down the wooden steps into the boat. Ron followed.

'Cup of tea?' asked Peggy.

'I could murder one,' he replied.

Tim picked up Freddie and stroked its head. 'Where are you off to?' he asked Ron.

'Only to Jean's shop,' he replied, 'to get some provisions.'

Peggy put Ron's tea on the table. She looked at Tim's empty mug. 'I suppose you want another one?'

He smiled. 'Is the Pope a Catholic?'

Ron blew on the tea to cool it down. 'Rose saw Smokey the other day. He's got Driftwood's ashes at the caravan but is unsure where to scatter them.'

Peggy sat down. 'Poor Smokey, it must be so hard for him, they were such good friends.'

# CHAPTER THREE

## The Letter

The high walls topped with razor wire of Her Majesty's Prison, Camp Hill, cast a gloomy shadow over the surrounding streets. Situated in the centre of the busy city, it housed Category C prisoners, meaning those who cannot be trusted in an open prison, but are unlikely to attempt an escape.

Inmate number 902 paced his small, white walled, single occupancy cell like a caged lion. Through the barred windows he could see the suffocating darkness being nudged aside by the coming dawn. For two years and nine months this grubby window had been his only view into the outside world. Now having served half his sentence he was being released on parole.

During his stay at Her Majesty's pleasure he had become 'useful' to one, Don Burns, a well-connected criminal serving four years for tax evasion and perjury. In prison terms 'useful' meant undertaking certain tasks, permitted or not, on behalf of your protector. In return your 'friendship' would not be forgotten either in jail or outside.

At eight o'clock on the dot, he heard the jangling of keys in the lock then the cell door was thrown open. He stepped out onto the landing on D wing. The officer searched him.

He chuckled. 'What the hell would I take out of here?'

Other prisoners, relieved that their nightly incarceration was over, scurried by on route to the showers and toilets. Some shouted to him.

'Good luck mate, give 'er a kiss from me!' Don Burns nodded as he passed him.

The surly officer led him in the opposite direction to them. At the bottom of a flight of metal steps they passed through two electronically controlled interconnecting doors. At the end of a green and cream painted corridor was a shabby, windowless room. On top of a wooden counter was a set of casual clothes, a pair of trainers and a jacket. He quickly changed out of the drab prison greys, his daily attire since arriving. The officer placed a plastic tray in front of him and told him to check the contents. He smiled as he recognised the items which had been taken from him at the start of his sentence. One lifeless mobile phone, a set of keys, one yellow disposable lighter, eight cigarettes in a crumpled packet, a ten-pound note and some assorted coins. Signing the form, he scooped up his only remaining worldly goods and put them in his pockets.

On the opposite side of the room was an open green door. He went through it and found himself in the yard next to the main gate. The officer spoke into his radio and seconds later the tall steel gates inched open. Standing on the road outside he stopped to inhale the fresh clean air of freedom, cleansing from his senses the smell of stale sweat and urine which had clung to him for the past one hundred and fifty-four weeks.

His mate Lee Finch, who had been released six months earlier, was waiting with a mini cab to take him to the hostel. They greeted each other with a hug as the heavy gates slammed shut. Ex prisoner 902 never looked back.

After leaving the home of the Barrington Gores, Ben had headed straight for Smokey Joe's place in Coote's Wood. He was part way through replacing the rotten wooden veranda at the front of the cottage. Smokey had been left the property by his uncle, the old Mr Coote who, for the last few years of his life, had become a recluse, allowing the cottage and surrounding grounds to fall into disrepair.

Smokey Joe had planned to live there with his friend, Driftwood. But Driftwood had died suddenly and his spirit had departed to Skiddledoor, the resting place of men of the road. Smokey was due to meet Ben at Coote's Wood at one o'clock, but had not yet left his caravan at Old Moor Lock. Not that it concerned him; everyone knew that Smokey Joe would be late for his own funeral. He had once told someone who had complained about his timekeeping, 'I'm never late, it's just that sometimes, I'm earlier than others.'

Driftwood's red bowler hat sat on the table alongside a simple plastic urn containing his ashes. Smokey shook his head at all that remained of his old roaming buddy. He picked up the urn and held it in front of him. 'So, what do you reckon me old mate? Should we keep the place or get rid of it?' He knew in his heart what Driftwood's reply would have been, but what was the point. If he was going to live alone again he might as well stay in the caravan, taking to the road whenever the mood took him.

He placed the urn back on the table and tapped the top. 'See you later mate.'
Putting on his long ex-army greatcoat, tied round the middle with string, and wide brimmed hat with pheasant's feather he left the caravan. Driftwood's old pram was still sitting underneath the window.

At a slow amble it would take him an hour to reach Coote's Wood, though he might stop for a cup of tea at Rocket Ron's boat on route.

The towpath at the edge of the woods was packed with boats moored alongside. When Smokey reached Old Moor Lock he sat on the wooden balance beam and closed his tired eyes.

Sleep had eluded him lately. A buttermilk sun brushed his cheek. The fragrance of freshly cut grass from the park opposite scented the morning air. A blend of birdsong and chattering ducks lifted his depressed mood.

His meditation though was disturbed by the clanking wheels of a loaded barrow being pushed by a red-faced puffing fisherman. Smokey smiled when he saw the amount of equipment needed to catch a fish. He stepped off the balance beam, ducked under the low bridge and onto the towpath below the lock. Now after the long winter there was new life on the canal; swans with their recently hatched cygnets inquisitively exploring their new world, ducks and moorhens, their chicks barely bigger than a fist, darting about behind them. A heron, its long neck just visible amongst the tall reeds waited patiently at the canal's edge.

At Wide Water he stopped to speak to a couple who had just flooded the lock chamber. Sitting on the bow end of the boat their young daughter cast a curious eye over Smokey's unusual attire. He smiled at her and walked on. He was used to it, having heard it all before.

'Is that man a tramp? Why is he dressed like a scarecrow?'

Hearing footsteps, he turned to find a pair of sweaty joggers bearing down upon him.

Flattening himself against the hedgerow he waited until the grim looking runners pounded by.'Why do they always look so miserable?' he thought to himself. He passed the swing bridge and rounded the long bend where the cows and horses came down to the water's edge to drink, then his nose started to twitch.

It was still a quarter of a mile before the sewage farm, known locally as the 'stink hole,' but already the unmistakable smell of freshly fermenting effluent was wafting towards him. At the side of the 'stink hole' was a small basin where several narrowboats were moored. It baffled Smokey why anybody would want to keep their boats in there. He hurried on. A lone kayaker came paddling towards him.

'Watch out for the swans,' he called. 'They have young with them.'

The young woman waved. 'Thanks, I will.' Recently several kayakers and paddle boarders had been attacked by the cobb and ended up in the water. At Springer's Lane Smokey viewed with disdain the acres of manicured greens of the new Japanese owned golf course, which until recently had been farmland. A new bridge across the canal carried punters to the hotel and spa complex. Opposite, in contrast to this manufactured sterility, were fields of bright yellow rapeseed. In the distance he could see Ron's boat moored astern of Rose's at Muckle Farm Bridge. If he were quick, he could snatch a cup of tea with him before going on to meet Ben at Coote's Wood.

Zed met Dwain outside the school gates just after three thirty. Although in the same year group they did not always share lessons. Zed had finished the school day with maths, taught by Mrs Peel, a softly spoken woman in her fifties. Whilst no doubt amply qualified in all things numerate, she had no such skills in controlling a class of teenagers, all yearning for the final bell to ring. This disruption though was nothing compared to the normal behaviour in the classroom at his old school in London. Dwain's last lesson was with Mr Steel. His subject, Geography, was taught with military precision, as would be expected from an ex-army officer.

The same group of youngsters who had boarded the bus earlier that day in Tiddledurn were waiting for its arrival. The tall girl with the long brown hair, looking as fresh as she did that morning, stood a few feet away talking to her friends. She turned to look in Dwain's direction. He smiled. Her look could have frozen water.

He nudged Zed. 'She's playing hard to get.'
Zed shook his head. 'You're wasting your time dude, she's out of your league.'
Dwain chuckled. 'We'll see about that.'

The school bus drew alongside the kerb and the automatic doors folded open. 'Hi guys, it's home time,' called the irritating driver, this time imitating an American accent. Again, everybody ignored him. Across from where Zed and Dwain sat, was the boy Dwain suspected of being the girl's brother. He and his friend were laughing loudly at something on Tik Tok. Dwain leant across the aisle.

'Hey man, is that girl at the back your sister?'
The boy half turned to look over his shoulder. 'Phoebe. Yes, that's right, we're twins,' he replied, in a clipped voice.

Dwain smiled. 'Cheer's mate. Oh, by the way I'm Dwain, this is Zed.'

The boy, slightly wary of these two London youngsters said, 'Oh, yes, right. I'm George, this is Eddie.'
The boy holding the phone nodded towards Dwain. 'Alright.'

Dwain sat back in the seat and whispered in Zed's ear. 'Got her name dude, it's Phoebe.'
Zed laughed. 'That's all you'll get mate.'

After leaving the bus in Tiddledurn, they would normally stop off to see Betty, Zed's gran, at the flat above the butcher's shop, before walking across the village green to Tim's cottage next to the canal. Tonight though, she was joining them for dinner and was already there. The green was busy with people walking dogs and shrieking kids in the playground. The boys, tired after their long day, slumped down on the wooden bench beside the duck pond. An elderly man sat opposite. Zed thought he looked sad. 'Must be horrible to be old and alone,' he said to Dwain.

Dwain agreed. 'I can't imagine being old.'
Zed took the remains of a curled-up sandwich from his bag and fed it to the ducks.

'The police have released Seaton and his mates,' he said suddenly.
Dwain looked shocked. 'What, how do you know?'
Zed shrugged. 'I just do.'
Dwain stood up; he was seething. 'After what they did to your gran's flat! Why are they free?'

'It's the system. They're on bail before the trial.'

'Then the system stinks,' shouted Dwain. 'Someone should wipe those smirks of their faces.'
Zed smiled. 'Maybe they will.'

'Does your gran know they're out?' asked Dwain.

Zed shook his head. 'No, and I don't want her to either.'

Dwain was still puzzled how Zed had found out but decided to leave it for now.

# CHAPTER FOUR

## Toss of a Coin

Before Smokey had time to knock on Rocket Ron's boat, the front doors opened and his two ferrets quickly scampered out. Smokey laughed as they jumped over the gunwales onto the towpath.

'Come in mate,' called Ron. 'I'll shove the kettle on.'

'Will they be alright?' asked Smokey, watching Frankie and Freddie who were now heading up the grass bank opposite.

Ron chuckled. 'They'll soon come in when the sparrow hawk sees them.'

Smokey took off his coat and hat and sat down at the small table.

'How you doing?' asked Ron.

Smokey sighed deeply. 'Not too bad, though I still miss the old devil.'

Ron did not need any reminding of how lonely living on your own can be. 'Life's a bitch,' he said. 'Just when things seem to be going right, she jumps up and bites you on the bum.'

Smokey laughed. 'I've certainly had plenty of bites there over the years.'

The two ferrets, bored with their ten minutes of freedom, came tumbling back through the front door. Ron shouted. 'Get in the cage, you pesky rodents.'

'So, have you decided what to do with Driftwood's ashes?' asked Ron, placing two mugs of tea on the table.

Smokey shook his head. 'Not really. I suppose the obvious place would be the woods by the caravan;

he liked it there. Ron agreed. 'You could ask Tim to make a wooden plaque, like he did for Barney.'

He nodded. 'Good idea mate.'

Ron went to a shelf, took down a plastic sleeve wallet and laid it on the table. 'Have you heard of Daisy Kearns?' he asked.

'No,' replied Smokey. 'Who is she?'

'Was,' replied Ron. He took from the sleeve three photocopies of newspaper articles printed in the Melbury Echo dated April 1943, which he had obtained recently from the local library.

Smokey studied one of the headlines. **'Land Army Girl Goes Missing from Muckle Farm'**

Ron said, 'It has always intrigued me what happened to her. I mean people can't just vanish, can they?'

'It says here the last sighting of her was at the Royal Oak pub,' observed Smokey, reading from the newspaper article.

Ron nodded. 'That's right. She had been drinking with some other Land Army girls and a few of the locals. Apparently, she left at ten o'clock to walk back to the farm, but never arrived.'

'Does seem odd,' agreed Smokey. 'Did the police investigation uncover anything?'

Ron shook his head. 'Zilch. Although it was wartime and resources were limited.'

Smokey grinned. 'Maybe she was a German spy?'

Ron laughed. 'Well, she wouldn't have learnt much at Muckle Farm.'

'There could have been secret military installations somewhere around here,' replied Smokey as he finished the last of his tea. 'Anyway Sherlock, I must be going. I was supposed to meet Ben at the cottage half an hour ago.' He stood up and put on his coat and hat.

'Are you going to keep the place?' asked Ron. Smokey smiled. 'Toss of a coin, my friend, toss of a coin,' and with that he was gone.

Ron watched him walk away along the towpath, his hunched shoulders looking as if the weight of the world was upon them.

Smokey stood for some time outside the gate leading into Coote's Wood. It would take only a few minutes to walk along the track to the cottage. A few minutes to make a life changing decision. He took a coin from his pocket, flipped it high into the air, caught it, then held it tightly in his fist.

Pushing open the gate he walked slowly, feeling every footstep as it connected with the rough surface. He stopped to look at the small stream which trickled alongside.

At the end of the track was a clearing with the overgrown remains of flower beds and lawns, once so lovingly tended by his aunt. The cottage, weathered and worn by age, stood in limbo between life and death. Renovation or demolition? Smokey sat down on a wooden bench, and raised his eyes towards Skidledoor, resting place for men of the road.

'Well, me old mate,' he said to Driftwood. 'It's decision time and I don't want any messages from white doves this time. Choose. Heads we keep it, tails it goes.' After a few minutes of sitting quietly he opened his fist. The head of Queen Elizabeth the Second was staring back at him.

Seeing Smokey sitting on the bench, Ben left the veranda and came over.

'I thought you'd forgotten me,' he said, sitting down.

'Yeah, sorry mate, got a bit waylaid.'

Ben looked concerned. 'Is there a problem?'

Smokey smiled. 'Not at all, Driftwood and me have sorted it.'

Ben seemed a little confused but said nothing.

Smokey stood up. 'Right, let's have a look at this veranda. I'm looking forward to sitting out here on summer evenings.'


The delivery from Willow Farm came promptly at seven o'clock every morning. Two dozen bottles of full cream milk and cartons of freshly laid eggs. Jean opened the front door of the canal shop as the small van drew up. Stan Jenkins, the farmer, and Jean had known each other since childhood. Like her he had inherited the business from his parents. Unlike her, he had married and produced two strapping sons, both now working on the farm. Stan opened the back doors of the van. He was still a handsome man, in a rugged sort of way, and she could understand why she had a crush on him at school.

'How's things going Jean?' He asked the same question every morning, and she always gave the same reply.

'Good, thanks Stan, everything's fine.'

But it was not and had not been for some time. She was getting older and running the shop on her own became more difficult with each day that passed. Having put the milk in the cooler and the eggs on the shelf, she went back outside and sat on the wooden bench next to Wills, her large black tom cat.

'I don't know what we're going to do,' she said to the purring puss.

A long lawn stretched from the shop to the canal's edge where there were six moorings for passing boats. On the opposite side of the canal were the old stables where the working boats of yesteryear would rest their towing horses overnight. Beyond that, standing like the scenery on a proscenium stage, the rounded, lush green hills of the Melbury Vale.

She was jarred from her contemplation by the shrill ringing of the telephone. Going through to the back room she lifted the receiver from the old-fashioned handset. She answered. A male voice, not of English origin asked, 'Is that Jean?' She replied it was. He apologised for ringing so early
in the morning and continued. 'My name is Jamel Goshi. My family own two convenience stores in and around Melbury. I understand that you may be selling your shop.'

His question took Jean completely by surprise. She paused. 'I think you must be mistaken.' Then she remembered mentioning to one of her suppliers that she might have to call it a day.

Jamel Goshi said, 'Oh, I am sorry to bother you but......'
Jean interrupted him. 'No, it's quite alright. You are partly correct, but I have yet to decide.'

'I understand,' he replied. 'But please take my number. As I said we would be interested in discussing it with you.'

She wrote his number on a notepad and promised to ring him back when and if she decided to sell. Wills had followed her in and sat on a chair waiting. It was his breakfast time.

'Well, what do you make of that Wills? Someone wants to buy us out.'

There was a loud gruff shout from the shop. 'Anyone there or is itself service now?'

She recognised the voice as Army Jim. Patting Wills on the head, she sighed. 'Maybe it's time.'


Tim knelt on the grass beside Odin and studied the rust along the waterline. He did the same with Thor. It had been four years since the hulls on both boats had been blacked, a procedure needed to protect the steel from rusting and pitting, and they urgently needed doing again. Unfortunately Harry Martin's marina did not have a dry dock. It would have to be Boswell's Yard which was some miles away. Their last journey there was not one he or Peggy would easily forget.

At the time she had been asked by Harry Martin to take one of his hire boats, Kingfisher, to Boswell's Yard for blacking. Having recently lost her own boat, Turtle, to fire and now living in a flat over the butcher's shop in Tiddledurn, she had been keen to oblige. Unbeknown to her, when she moored at Jean's canal shop to buy provisions, eleven-year-old Zed, who had fled from the circus, had stowed away on the boat.

It was some miles further on when she had discovered the grubby, tearful boy hiding in a wardrobe. The poor lad was panic stricken that he would be sent back to his exploitative uncle at the circus. Unsure what to do with him and mindful of the tight deadline to arrive a Boswell's Yard, Peggy had rung Tim. Eventually with the help of Mrs Phillips, the headteacher of the village school in Tiddledurn, they had managed to contact Zed's gran, Betty, in London. After much discussion it was decided that Zed would stay on the boat for the remainder of the trip then Mrs Phillip's husband would take him back to London. Mindful of losing the dry dock slot Tim had agreed to go with them.

Tim went down into the stern skipper's cabin on Odin and looked at the picture which Peggy had taken of him and Zed fishing on the canal bank during that week. He smiled to himself. Little did either of them realise then how future events would evolve and what an impact Zed and his friend, Dwain, would have on their lives. As he wandered back along the towpath towards the cottage, he contemplated how he could schedule in taking the boats to Boswell's Yard. He had a full diary of work to be completed on people's boats and could not afford to let them down, in addition to Harry Martin's hire fleet which needed constant maintenance.

The front door of the cottage was open. He went inside but there was no sign of Peggy. Then he heard music coming from the 'shepherd's hut' which he had bought for her last year. Zed and Dwain called it a 'shed on wheels.' Walking around the side of the cottage he climbed the three wooden steps. Instantly he could smell the paints and lacquers she used to create her Canal Art.

Often referred to as Castles and Roses, it originated in the nineteenth century when waterways folk decorated their boats in cheerful chocolate box colours. Peggy concentrated on items which could be sold to passing tourists or boat hirers, such as Buckby Cans, tea pots, mugs, and plates. She had learned the skill as a girl from a working boatman and his wife who frequently travelled through Tiddledurn on their way to load or off load at the docks.

'Knock, knock,' he called, pushing open the green door. Inside Peggy was sitting on a stool carefully painting a yellow flower onto a plate. 'Very nice,' said Tim. 'I couldn't have done better myself.'

She raised her eyes. 'You're too ham fisted to paint anything delicate.'

He looked at his large leathery hands and nodded. 'You're probably right.'

'So, to what do I owe this visit?' she asked. 'I thought you'd gone to the boats.'

He pulled up another stool and sat next to her. 'I need to get the boats to Boswell's for blacking.'

'Are they due?' asked Peggy.

He laughed. 'They're overdue.'

Peggy put down the brush. 'Are you asking me if I can take them?'

He shrugged. 'I'm bogged down with work Peg and I can't let people down.'

Peggy thought for a moment. 'Normally I would say yes. But I'm reluctant to leave Betty, particularly while she's feeling so vulnerable.'

Tim nodded. 'I can see that.' He stood up. 'Oh well, I'll see what I can work out.'

As he reached the door she called to him. 'Tim, there is another option.'

He turned. 'What's that?'

'Let Zed and Dwain take them,' she answered.

'What?' he exclaimed loudly. 'Are you serious?'

'I am,' she replied calmly. 'They're nearly sixteen and as you have said yourself, they can handle the boats really well.'

Tim stammered. 'I know Peg, but……'

'But nothing,' she replied. 'What's the worse they can do? After all, you taught them all they know.'

He couldn't argue with that. 'I'll think about it,' he replied.

Peggy called after him. 'You need to let go a bit more; you're not getting any younger.'

He came back, put his head round the door and grinned. 'Makes two of us my love.'

She poked her tongue out at him.

# CHAPTER FIVE

## The Quest

### MELBURY ECHO April 21st, 1943

*One week on and, despite an extensive search of the surrounding area by the police and local people, the disappearance of Daisy Kearns, the Land Army girl from Muckle Farm, remains a mystery. Kearns, twenty-four and originally from South London, was last seen in the public bar of the Royal Oak in Tiddledurn drinking with other Land Army girls and villagers. She left the bar to walk back to Muckle Farm at ten o'clock but never arrived home. Detective Inspector Brian Fawcett who is leading the investigation is appealing for any witnesses who may have seen her after leaving the Royal Oak Public House.*

### MELBURY ECHO 28th APRIL 1943

*The police have confirmed that following last week's appeal in this newspaper regarding the disappearance of Land Army Girl, Daisy Kearns, a witness has come forward claiming that a girl matching her description was seen by the telephone box in Porchester Street at ten fifteen. Enquiries are on-going.*

After Smokey Joe had left the boat Rocket Ron studied these and subsequent articles with interest. In the following May editions of 1943, barely a line was being reported in the Echo on the disappearance of Daisy Kearns.

'Enquiries are on-going?' he muttered to himself.

But they were not. Like many local crimes they had become casualties of the inferno of war now raging across Europe and the ever-present threat of invasion by the Nazis to this country. He took a pink highlighter from the drawer and marked up certain pieces of the text. Drumming his fingers on the table, he said out loud. 'There must be records somewhere of these girls and their original addresses.'

He took out his phone and rang the local newspaper. A pleasant female voice answered.

'Good afternoon, the Melbury Echo. Which Department do you require?'

Ron asked to be put through to the editorial team. There was a pause whilst a piece of obscure classical music played. Ron thought he recognised it from some old television advert, but he was not sure. A male voice answered.

'Hi, editorial, how can I help?'

Ron deduced that he was talking to a young man. He explained to him that he was trying to track down someone featured in an article.

The editorial assistant asked. 'Ok sir, which edition was it in?'

Ron braced himself. 'April 21st, 1943.'

There was a brief silence. 'Sorry did you say 1943?' he asked.

Ron smiled. 'I did.'

'I'll have to put you on hold for a second,' said the young man. The previous automated piece of music again filled the otherwise silent void.

After what seemed an age another female voice, more mature than the first, came on the line.

'Hello, sorry to keep you waiting. I'm Sharon Giddings, the editor. I'm afraid we don't keep records dating back to that period. What exactly are you trying to find?' Ron explained that he had obtained photocopies from the library of the articles the Echo had run about Daisy Kearns' disappearance and was hoping the paper might have retained further information on her, or the case.

'Unfortunately not,' she replied. 'You could try the National Archives at Kew in London. They would hold the details of all serving personnel of that era including the Land Army. But you would have to visit them, there are no online records.' Ron thanked her. She wished him luck.

'Keep in touch,' the editor asked, 'could be a future story here.'
He said he would.

He switched off the mobile phone then called to the two ferrets who were still obediently lying in their cage. 'Come on rodents, let's go and see Rose.' He left the boat and walked the short distance along the towpath. Frankie and Freddie ran ahead in anticipation of a treat which Rose always gave them. He looked at the dulled and peeling paintwork on Rose's boat. Like his own it could do with sprucing up, but neither of them had the energy to do it themselves, or the money to pay someone else. Bending down he tightened up the slack bow and stern mooring lines.

Rose had risen early that day before going into the woods to collect the herbs she needed to make her healing potions. Through the open windows Ron could smell the pungent boiling mixture. He winced at the thought of drinking the bitter brew, but it seemed to be helping his arthritic knees, so he would hold his nose and reluctantly swallow it down.

'Come in,' she called. 'I'm just finishing your remedy.'

He sat down in a battered armchair. Frankie and Freddie stood staring at a shelf where Rose kept the jar with the small crunchy dog biscuits in. She removed the lid, took out a handful and threw them on the floor. The two ferrets tumbled over each other to eat the most biscuits.

Ron shook his head. 'Look at them, you would think they were never fed.'

'I have a favour to ask,' he said.

She laughed. 'I have no money.'

He chuckled. 'Oh, and here was I thinking you were loaded!'

'So, what is it?' she asked, stirring the herbal brew.

'Would you be able to have Frankie and Freddie one day whilst I go to London?'

She turned round. 'What in God's name do you want to go there for?'

'I'm on a quest,' he replied.

'Ah, our very own <u>Frodo Baggins</u>,' she said removing the hot pot from the stove.

He chuckled. 'Nothing so dramatic, my precious. I'm going to the National Archive in Kew, to see if I can find out more about that Land Army Girl, Daisy Kearns.'

She sighed. 'I've heard about that. Poor girl; another casualty of that awful war.'  ,

Ron shrugged. 'Well, we're only assuming she was killed, anything could have happened to her.'

'When are you going?' she asked.

'Not sure,' he replied. 'I need to check the coach times from Melbury. It'll be cheaper than going by train.'

He watched her as she poured the cooling liquid into a large mug. A slight tremor shook her hand. It saddened him to see it. She was so thin now, her long fine hair as white as snow. How different from the young, carefree hippy girl he had met selling homemade jewellery on the towpath all those years ago. But then these days he hardly recognised himself when he looked in the mirror.

She placed the mug in front of him. He winced at the thought of drinking it.

'How are the bears?' he asked trying to delay the moment.

She sat down in the chair opposite him. 'I'm just waiting for the full moon, then I can put them all around the bear tree and they can dance and dance until dawn breaks.'

He smiled. Amongst other things, it was this mild eccentricity which he had always loved about her.

She tapped the mug with her finger. 'Come on, drink up like a good boy.'

Slowly he put the mug to his lips then, like a sky diver making his first jump into the unknown, closed his eyes and quickly swallowed it down. His face contorted with pure revulsion.

Rose smiled. 'There, that wasn't too bad, was it?'

His expression said otherwise.

The boys had not been at Melbury Academy long, before Dwain clocked Tommy Hitch. He was a bully who, along with his little posse of mates, liked to push the younger pupils around and, if they could get away with it,

those in their own year group too. He had steered clear of Zed and Dwain, his provincial instincts warning him not to chance it with two kids fresh from the streets of South London, particularly Dwain who had developed into quite a muscular teenager.

Overlooking the football and rugby pitches behind the main building of the school was a grassy knoll. It was a popular place for the students to gather during break times. Zed and Dwain sat together at the end of the knoll where it tapered towards the freshly mown sports fields.

'Bit different to our school in London,' said Zed, looking out across the green expanse, the view only blemished by a new housing estate of red brick boxes. Dwain agreed and passed him a handful of jelly babies. He was addicted to them, buying a large bag every morning in Tiddledurn before boarding the school bus.

Further along the knoll, a group of youngsters were grazing peacefully on the contents of their lunch boxes. Amongst them were the twin brother and sister, Zed and Dwain now knew as George and Phoebe.

It was the female voice shouting, 'Stop it you idiots!'
which made Dwain and Zed turn to look. Tommy
Hitch and his mates had sat down a few feet away and
were throwing handfuls of freshly mown grass at them.
As Phoebe angrily brushed the grass from her hair,
her brother George stood up to confront the larger
Tommy Hitch.

Dwain and Zed couldn't hear what was said
between them but suddenly Hitch shoved George hard
in the chest, sending him falling backwards down the
knoll. Phoebe stood up and yelled at the pack of
laughing hyenas. Then just as George was getting to his
feet,
Hitch leapt upon him pinning his body to the ground.
Dwain had seen enough. 'Stay there,' he said to Zed.

He ran the short distance towards the now
scattered group. Launching himself onto Tommy Hitch
he knocked him sideways off George and onto the
grass. Before he could react, Dwain was on top, holding
him down and twisting his tie tightly around his neck.
Hitch coughed and spluttered as Dwain tightened his
grip. His gobby cowardly mates looked on unsure what
to do.

Dwain bent close to his sweaty, reddening face.
'This is your first and last warning dude. Go near them
again and I swear to God I will fill your sinuses with
urine.' Dwain had heard this term being used in a
gangster film he and Zed were watching one night on
Turtle. He poked him in the chest. 'You get me man?'
he shouted, putting on his best imitation 'Jamaican
rude boy' voice. Humiliated and defeated Hitch
nodded meekly.

Dwain released his grip on Hitch's tie and stood up. Without a sideways glance Hitch and his mates skulked quickly away.

George came over to him. 'Cheers Dwain. He caught me completely by surprise.'

Dwain smiled. 'Any time mate.'

Zed had been watching all this from a distance. Whilst admiring his friend's bravado he had been ready to intervene if the pack of hyenas had joined in, but they had not, so he stayed where he was. As Dwain turned to walk back to where Zed was sitting, Phoebe called to him. He turned. 'Thank you,' she said, kissing him on the cheek. He blushed. As she walked away, he was riveted to the ground as a tsunami of hormones flooded through his teenage body.

Zed tapped him on the shoulder. 'Come on, the bell's gone.'

'She kissed me, did you see?' said Dwain, still in a daze.

Zed laughed. 'Yeah, I did. Eat some more jelly babies and cool down.'

Unbeknown to any of them the incident on the knoll had been watched from an upstairs window by the Head of Year eleven Mrs Greta Holmesbran. Whilst there had been several complaints about the behaviour of Tommy Hitch and his acolytes, none had ever been witnessed by a member of staff, until now. Before that day was over, they would feel the searing heat from the mouth of the one they called 'The Dragon Lady.'

# CHAPTER SIX

## Revenge

In South London, The Old Kent Road was as different from the so called 'Garden of England' as chalk is to cheese. On either side of this busy polluted artery, rows of grubby run-down shops huddled together. Standing amongst them between the Thomas-a-Beckett pub and a newsagent was a popular Turkish kebab shop.

Inside this hot and brightly lit eatery three men, Bradley Seaton, Ryan Sharp, and Ashley Green sat next to the window on plastic stools. Behind the glass display counter, a young man of Turkish descent carved from a rotating cone shaped mass of pressed meat.

'You want chilli sauce?' he called, as he pushed the thin slices into a piece of opened pitta bread.

Seaton nodded. 'Yeah mate.'

The other two had finished their doner kebab earlier and were drinking from cold cans of cola. Ryan Sharp checked the time on his mobile phone, it was six thirty. They had less than three hours of freedom, before the electronic tags they wore on their ankles would alert police that they were in breach of the nine o'clock bail curfew, leading to their arrest.

The conversation between them was subdued, particularly Sharp and Green, whose complicity in Seaton's act of revenge on Betty, Zed's gran, was no doubt going to lead to a substantial prison sentence. Seaton playing the hard man shrugged off his impending stay at Her Majesty's pleasure, still maintaining the old bird had deserved it. None of them had noticed the dark green Audi with tinted glass windows parked against the kerb on the opposite side of the road. For the second day running its two North London occupants had been monitoring the trio's movements. Outside the streetlights flickered on as the evening rush hour traffic from the city started to ease. Seaton finished the last mouthful of his kebab, wiped a hand across his mouth, sniffed loudly then threw the carton in the bin.

'Come on, let's go,' he said, sliding off the stool. Despite everything which had transpired of late Green and Sharp still hung on his every word. Pulling up their hoodies they left the takeaway and went out onto the gum spattered pavement.

Inside the parked green Aldi, the observant driver lowered his window and lit a cigarette.

'They're leaving,' he said to the man next to him who was lying back in the passenger seat with his eyes closed. Saying nothing, he zipped up his jacket and stepped out of the car. Waiting for a gap in the traffic he quickly crossed the road in pursuit of the three slouching figures. A short distance past the Thomas-a-Becket pub, famous as the training venue for heavyweight boxer Henry Cooper, they turned off into one of several small terraced streets named after historic military figures; Wellington, Nelson, Wolfe, and Cromwell. Having walked this way many times before, Nelson was the only historic name they could relate too, and although they knew his statue stood high in Trafalgar Square, they had no idea why.

This short cut would lead them past Surrey Quays, one of the old London docks, now a water sports centre and shopping mall. From there it was only a short distance to the Rotherhithe Road.

Walking slowly with hardly a word spoken between them they headed towards their high-rise homes on the housing estate opposite the Rotherhithe Tunnel. The fire blackened external walls of Betty's flat on the eight floor of Nelson House were still visible from the ground.

From a discrete distance the North London Audi man watched as the hunched hoodies jumped over the low wall onto the bald grass which bounded the estate. After monitoring which block each man went in to, he took out his mobile phone and texted the driver to pick him up. His reconnaissance was complete. Now he would wait. As was usual, the order from Don Burns in Camp Hill Prison would be sent in one of three coded messages. 'Say hello to Ted, say hello to Horace' or 'Say hello to Lennie.' This would indicate the level of action to be taken.

Tim had been working at Harry Martin's marina since early morning. He stood back and admired the new central heating system which he had just fitted into Heron, one of the hire boats.

'That's a good job, I say that's a good job,' said Harry, suddenly appearing on the pontoon behind him. Harry always repeated everything twice. Tim wiped his hand on an oily rag.

'Good heaters these, better than those old things you had in there.'
Harry laughed. 'Only three more boats to go, I say only three more.'
Tim sighed. 'Tell me about it. Anyway, that's for another day, now I need a brew.'

Harry's office, with adjoining kitchen, was adjacent to the service point where boats could moor alongside to fill up with fuel or pump out the toilets. Inside the cluttered room Tim moved a pile of brochures before plonking himself down wearily into a chair.

Harry emerged from the kitchen with two mugs of tea and a packet of biscuits.

'So, how's things going?' asked Harry, sitting down at the desk. 'I say how's things?'

Tim shook his head. 'Well let's just say it would be easier for me if you had a dry dock, then I wouldn't have to take the boats all that way to Boswell's Yard for blacking.'

Harry dunked a biscuit into his tea. 'When are you going? I say when.........?'

Tim interrupted him before he finished the question. 'That's the problem, I haven't really got the time to take them.'

Harry thought for a moment. 'What about the boys? I say what about Zed and Dwain?'

Tim shook his head. 'I know. That's what Peggy said, but........'

This time Harry interrupted him. 'I would trust them with my boats, I say I would trust them.'

Tim sighed deeply. 'You may be right,' he chuckled, not being able to resist. 'I say you may be right.'

Harry laughed loudly. 'Don't mock the afflicted. I say don't knock.......'


Arriving back home Tim parked the Land Rover at the back of the cottage. He groaned as he lifted his weighty toolbox from the back of the old Series One workhorse and carried it inside his workshop. A large wooden structure, it was an Aladdin's cave of tools, engine parts and maintenance equipment.

The space was dominated by a heavy wooden work bench with a large vice secured to the surface. Once they left school it would also become a classroom for Zed and Dwain as their training in boat engineering commenced. This would be supplemented by one day a week at Melbury Further Education College, and work experience at Harry Martin's marina.

Tim was looking forward to the day when Zed and Dwain could take on more of this work; crawling about in engine compartments was becoming more difficult for him. As Peggy had mischievously pointed out to him recently, 'You're not getting any younger.'

He went into the kitchen to make a brew. Peggy had gone to see Betty in her flat over the butcher's shop in Tiddledurn and the boys had already hunkered down for the evening on Turtle.

Next to the microwave was a cottage pie and some vegetables for him to heat up. Outside the sun was sinking slowly to the horizon and the day's light ebbing away. Taking his mug of strong tea into the garden he sat down on the grass beside Barney's grave.

'So, what do you reckon Barney, should we let the boys take the boats to Boswell's yard on their own?' Unlike Smokey who was convinced Driftwood's soul resided in Skidledoor, Tim had no idea where Barney's spirit was. But if there was a doggy heaven then he knew Barney would be there. He watched a young grey squirrel swinging from a high branch like a trapeze artist. No safety net required here.

It was not that he did not trust Zed and Dwain, he was more concerned for their safety if anything went wrong. Reflecting on Peggy's words, 'What's the worst that can happen?' he shuddered.

Over the years he had heard of and witnessed some awful accidents and damage on the waterways, particularly to people using boats from hire companies.

'You have a think about it and let me know mate,' he said, touching the wooden plaque he had so lovingly carved. 'We'll talk later.'

Turtle rocked gently against its mooring. On the sofa, dressed only in a pair of blue shorts, Dwain pulled a cushion over his head and let out a muffled scream. 'Why do we get so much homework at this school?' Zed laughed. Even if he did want to help him, he could not, as he was hopeless at science.

'I'm going for a walk,' Zed announced, leaving him writhing in frustration. As he opened the door, he cast a sideways glance at Dwain's dark athletic body.

He walked along the towpath to where Odin and Thor were moored. A bat, awoken by the dying of the light, swooped close to his head. He unclipped a section of the canvas roof enabling him to climb down the steps inside Odin. It smelt clean and fresh after Peggy's recent onslaught with bottles of bleach. This was the first opportunity he had to be on his own. Sitting on one of the maroon-coloured plastic mattresses he took from his pocket the letter he had received some days ago. Again, he read through the spidery text littered with simple spelling mistakes. At the bottom of the page alongside a mobile phone number and a greasy thumbprint it was signed off. 'Please call me mate, Darren.'

Zed cringed at the thought of having to speak with his uncle again, particularly after his treatment by him at the circus and his attempt to steal the Golden Windlass from Rose. But there was a burning pain deep inside his young body, which no amount of medication could ever extinguish. Since the day he was born, the one constant person who had unconditionally loved him the most, his gran Betty, had been grievously hurt and he felt that deeply.

One word highlighted in capital letters stood out amongst the others. 'REVENGE.' It was a weighty word. He rolled the harsh sounding verb around his mouth before loudly emphasizing the two syllables RE - VENGE to the roomy interior. Of course, he had heard the word used many times in films and on television, such as, 'Revenge of the Jedi' or 'Revenge of the Green Dragon,' and he knew that the eventual outcome for people was nearly always unpleasant.

Knowing in his heart that neither Gran nor Peggy or Tim would agree with the content of the letter, or his complicity in it, he momentarily let his hand hover over the screen of his mobile phone. Then he tapped in Darren's number. The voice that answered was flat. Any arrogant cockiness which Zed remembered from his mother's brother had gone.

'Allo.'
At first Zed said nothing.

'Allo, who's this?' the voice demanded sharply.
Cautiously he answered. 'It's me, Zed.'
Darren chuckled. 'Zed, me little nephew, 'ow are you mate?'

'Alright thanks,' said Zed. 'You?'
Darren coughed, a chesty smoker's bark. 'Yeah, I'm doing good, now I'm out of that 'ell 'ole.'
Zed did not offer a reply. As far as he was concerned, Darren had deserved every day of his imprisonment.

'So, you got me letter?' asked Darren.
Zed said he had.

'And?' he asked. 'Are you up for it? Teach those three a lesson they won't forget.'

He sensed Zed's reluctance to answer. 'You 'aven't got to do anything.'

'What does it matter if I agree or not?' asked Zed.

He laughed. 'Cos it matters dude. I'm doing this for you and Mum. What would 'ave 'appened if you 'ad been in there when they tipped petrol through the letterbox?'

Zed knew he was right. He hated Bradley Seaton, Ryan Sharp, and Ashley Green for what they had done to his gran.

Darren pressed on. 'So, what do you reckon dude, shall we burn their fingers?'

Zed was quiet as he detected a rising excitement in his uncle's voice. Was this a manifestation of revenge?

'You there Zed?' he asked curtly.

Zed held his finger over the red button, then said. 'Do what you like.' Before Darren could reply he terminated the call. He made several attempts to call Zed back, but they were all ignored.

# CHAPTER SEVEN

## Classified

The following morning Betty met Peggy on the village green, and they walked along the canal side to Jean's shop. As they approached the gate at the bottom of the garden, Army Jim stood menacingly on the towpath next to his boat. A long-bladed sheath less machete hung from his belt. As usual he was dressed from top to toe in army camouflaged clothing. It was difficult to decide if his facial skin was tanned by the sun or streaked with dirt. Noticing the black under his long fingernails Peggy concluded it was probably a bit of both. Betty, who was next to her, had never seen such a creature before and was a little disturbed by his size and scowling manner.

'Hello Jim,' said Peggy. 'You're still moored here then?'
He grunted and stepped back so they could access the gate. Betty hurried by without making any eye contact. They were part way across the lawn towards the shop when there was a slurred shout.
'Oi, Sheaintthur.'
The rapid broad West Country accent was difficult to understand. Both women turned.
'What did he say?' asked Betty.
Peggy shrugged. 'Say it again Jim.'
'Sheaintthur. Jean, Sheaintthur.'
This time Peggy understood. 'Do you know where she is?'
He shrugged.

'

Peggy checked her watch. It was ten past ten. 'Something's wrong. She wouldn't leave the shop closed without telling someone.' They quickened their pace towards the shop. The door was still locked and the curtains in the upstairs windows closed. Whilst Betty went to check the back door, Peggy rang Jean's mobile. It went straight to voicemail.

Peggy banged loudly on the door and called her name, but there was still no response from inside. Betty returned from the rear of the shop. 'It's locked too,' she said.

'We'll have to break in,' said Peggy.

'Are you quite sure she wouldn't have just gone somewhere?' asked Betty.

Peggy was just about to answer when a loud meowing from Jean's tom cat came from behind the door. Peggy pushed open the letterbox. 'Hello Wills, it's Peggy. We won't be a moment.'

She turned to Betty. 'There is no way she would leave Wills locked up inside if she went out.'

Both women looked around for something they could use to smash the glass with. There was not much but eventually Betty found a reasonable sized stone. Peggy took off her scarf, wrapped it around her hand then took the weapon from Betty. Carefully selecting a spot on the glass nearest to the inside door lock she drew back the stone, then as she was about to strike a vice like grip seized her arm.

'Moveouttheway,' Army Jim said abruptly, as he pulled his long machete from his leather belt. The two women stood back. Inserting the pointed end of the thick blade between the door and the frame he levered hard on the handle.

There was a sound of splintering as the lock reluctantly retreated from the wood. He inspected his handywork, then gave another firm tug on the machete and the door opened. Wills shot out onto the grass. Jim stood aside so Peggy and Betty could enter.

The well-stocked shop was in darkness. Only the gentle hum of the chiller units broke the silence. Betty pulled up the window blinds. Peggy located the light switch behind a rotating display unit containing sunglasses. The fluorescent bulbs overhead flashed on, illuminating the interior. She looked behind the counter and into the small stock room. At the rear of the shop was Jean's living accommodation. Apprehensive as to what she might find Peggy slowly opened the dividing door.

The small comfortable room with its adjoining kitchen, was as neat and tidy as always, with no signs of anything unusual having occurred. Betty pointed to a bottle of sleeping tablets on the table. The stairs leading to the two bedrooms were narrow with threadbare carpets. Peggy started to ascend the creaky steps. On reaching the landing she pushed open the door next to the bathroom which she knew was Jean's bedroom.

In the dimly lit room, she could make out a still shape in the double bed. Betty followed her in and drew back the curtains. Peggy, now fearful of the outcome, gently shook the duvet clad body.
She called out. 'Jean, Jean.' There was no response. Peggy pulled back the duvet and to her immense relief Jean was still breathing. Again, she called her name, and this time shook her a little harder.

Jean stirred, mumbled something then slowly opened her eyes. 'What? Where? Peggy, why are you here?' She reached out for the alarm clock on the bedside table, then dropped it on the floor. 'What time is it?' she asked.

Peggy laughed. 'It's gone eleven.'

Jean blinked furiously. 'Oh my god, the shop! I have to open up.'

Peggy put her hands on her shoulders. 'You don't have to do anything, stay there and rest.'

'I'll go and make a nice cup of tea,' said Betty. Jean lifted herself up against the pillows. 'I must have taken too many of those sleeping tablets.'

Peggy smiled. 'You certainly had us worried dear.'

'How did you get in?' she asked.

'I'm afraid we had to break in the front door.' Jean sighed. 'I'm such a fool. I was so tired, I just needed to get some sleep.'

Betty arrived back with three cups of tea. Wills followed her and jumped up onto the bed.

'He's glad to see you,' said Peggy. Jean stroked the purring puss. 'I expect you want your breakfast, don't you?'

There was the sudden sound of slow, heavy footsteps coming from the creaky stairway. Jean gasped as the looming figure of Army Jim filled the bedroom doorway. She quickly pulled the duvet up tight around her neck.

'Youalrightnow?' he said gruffly.

Jean smiled. 'I am. Thank you Jim.'

Peggy said, 'We have Jim to thank for getting us in.'

'Oh really!' exclaimed Jean. 'Well, thank you again.'

Army Jim suddenly pulled the long machete from his belt and held it upright in front of him.

'MeandSlasherere.' He ran his thumb along the thin blade. 'Verysharp,' he said with a crooked smile. Jean turned to Peggy. 'I'll get up now just in case there are any customers.'

Peggy replied firmly. 'I think you should stay closed today and rest. We'll wait downstairs for you.'

Army Jim went out through the shop and sat on the wooden bench outside, the machete visible to anyone approaching.

Peggy laughed. 'That'll stop any potential customers in their tracks.'

Betty gave a wry smile. 'If I didn't know better, I would say he has a soft spot for her.'

Peggy was aghast at the thought. 'Good grief, don't tell her that. She'll freak out.'

Both women laughed. Betty made another pot of tea and they sat down at the table.

'So, what's troubling Jean?' asked Betty. Peggy gestured around the room. 'This place, she's getting older and finding it much harder to run the shop on her own.'

'Can't she employ an assistant?' asked Betty. Peggy shook her head. 'She did advertise for someone part time but can only afford to pay the minimum wage. There was one applicant, a student, she only lasted a week. To be honest Jean has never been the same since the break in. It was a terrible shock for her.'

'Yes, I remember Zed telling me about it,' replied Betty. 'Poor woman.'

Rocket Ron stood in front of the National Archives building in Kew, having arrived earlier that morning at

Victoria Coach Station. It had been forty years since he had visited London and he had forgotten just what a bustling place the metropolis was. A simple country boy, he was slightly intimidated by the intensity of the huge seventies architecture which stood before him. He did though find comfort in the surrounding scenic gardens and lake with its familiar marine wildlife.

Taking a deep breath, he entered the building through a glass sliding door. Once inside he stood at the edge of a colourfully decorated open plan foyer. At its centre was a highly polished, circular wooden structure, above which hung a vivid sign saying. 'Welcome Desk.' He approached one of the four receptionists, a tall middle-aged woman.

'How can I help?' she asked, smiling, which immediately put him at ease.
Feeling less apprehensive Ron produced the Melbury Echo newspaper cuttings, placed them on the counter and explained the purpose of his visit. She picked them up and for several minutes read through them.

'How interesting, quite a detective story,' she said, handing them back. 'Now let us see if we can find you a reference.' Sitting down in front of a computer screen, she asked. 'You did say 1943?'

Ron nodded. 'That's right.'

Slowly and methodically, she started to scroll through pages of data. Every so often she would remove her glasses, wipe them on a cloth and replace them onto her nose. She tapped the screen with her pen.

'Here we are. Tiddledurn, a village near Melbury. Land Army movements and personnel 1940 - 1944.' She pressed another button on the keyboard. 'That will be under the South West Region: Sector 5.'

Taking a slip of pink paper from off the desk she wrote on it. Password. KIWI 23, Reference code, TX421, then handed it to Ron. She pointed across the foyer to a set of heavy double doors.

'You will find computers on the desks. Enter the password, then key in the reference code.
All the information relating to your enquiry will then be available to you.'

Sensing he was not the most computer savvy of people, she smiled. 'Don't worry there is an assistant in there to help you.'

He thanked her, took the slip of paper and headed across the spacious foyer towards Reading Room One.

'Good luck,' she called after him.

There were two workstations available; he sat down at the nearest one. Looking around him the studious clientele were all silently absorbed in their research, with only the sound of tapping keyboards breaking the monastic silence. He was approached by a young man who introduced himself as Toby. 'Are you ok? he asked.

Ron chuckled. 'I would be if I knew how to switch it on.'

Toby laughed, pressed a button on the side of the computer and the screen illuminated. Pulling up a chair, he asked Ron to show him the pink reference slip he had been given. His fingers moved rapidly across the keypad.

'There we are,' he said pointing to the screen. 'Reference TX421. Land Army movements and personnel 1940 - 1944. Southwest Region.' Ron thanked him.

Toby stood up. 'We can't print anything off, but feel free to take whatever notes you require. If you need any help, give me a call.'

Ron pulled his chair tight into the desk. Taking an exercise book from his pocket he laid it next to the computer. The next two hours passed quickly as he scrolled through pages and pages of text, stopping occasionally to make notes in his book. There was though one document unavailable to him. Highlighted in red were just four words. 'OPERATION GREEN FIELDS, RESTRICTED.'

Ron called Toby over to explain. He studied the highlighted text.

'It's classified information. Need to know only.' Chuckling, he said, 'James Bond 007 territory I'm afraid.'

Ron shrugged. 'What, after all this time?' Toby nodded. 'A lot of Second World War stuff still is.'

After leaving the building through the sliding glass doors, Ron sat on a bench overlooking the sparkling lake. He checked his watch. It was two thirty in the afternoon and he was hungry. That morning Rose had prepared him a packed lunch. Taking the flask from his bag he poured a cup of tea, then pulling the exercise book from his pocket mulled over his handwritten notes. At the bottom of the last page, he had written in capital letters, 'Operation Green Fields.'

'Now what was that all about?' he said loudly to himself.

# CHAPTER EIGHT

## Secrets

Still feeling a little drowsy from the effect of the sleeping tablets, Jean carefully descended the creaky stairs from her bedroom. Wills followed her down.

'Ah, sleepy bones,' said Peggy, as she came into the small living room at the rear of the shop.

Jean laughed, 'I'm lucky it wasn't a permanent sleep.' She went to the cupboard, took out a sachet of cat food, mixed it with some dried biscuits and emptied it into Will's bowl. He attacked it as if he had been starved for a month.

As she sat down at the table with Betty and Peggy, Army Jim, looking like a veteran commando, called from inside the shop. ' Illbeoffnow.'

'Do you need anything while you're here?' asked Jean.

'Noimalrighttiltommorow,' he answered, heading off.

'He's a kind soul underneath all that gruffness and grime,' said Peggy.

Jean agreed then said, 'I have something to tell you. I've had an offer on the shop.'

Shocked by the sudden announcement, Peggy asked, 'Offer! What offer? From who?'

'A Mr Jamel Goshi, his family run a convenience store in Melbury.'

'But this is all you have ever known Jean; it's your life. You can't sell it.'

Jean chuckled. 'If I carry on like this Peg, I won't have much life left.'

Peggy shook her head. 'There has to be another way. What about all your canal customers? You would be dreadfully missed, and anyway, where would you live?'

'I could get a small flat somewhere in Tiddledurn or Melbury,' Jean replied.

Peggy laughed mockingly. 'And what about Jack? Are you going to keep him on the balcony? The neighbours will love that!'

Poor Jean was getting exasperated with her old friend. 'What else can I do Peggy? It's all too much.'

Suddenly there was a loud and angry squawking noise from outside.

'Good grief,' said Betty, startled.

Jean smiled. 'Jack probably wants his breakfast too.' She went into the kitchen, took a scoop of food from a plastic bin then went out through the back door. Peggy and Betty followed. With outstretched neck and flapping wings, the goose raced towards the surrounding wire fence. Jean undid the gate. 'Get back Jack,' she shouted, pushing her way into the pen.

'Rather her than me,' chuckled Betty.

'He's gentle really. Unless you're a cyclist,' replied Peggy, laughing.

Betty was not convinced.

Whilst Jean was feeding Jack and refilling his drinking trough Betty beckoned Peggy back inside. 'I have an idea which might help out,' she said.

Intrigued, Peggy asked, 'What?'

Betty sat down at the table. 'Why don't I help Jean in the shop for a few days a week?'

The suggestion took Peggy completely by surprise. 'Would you Betty? Are you sure about it?'

Betty laughed. 'Well, I hardly have a packed diary do I?'

Peggy took hold of Betty's hand. 'Oh, that would be wonderful, just wonderful.'

'What's wonderful?' asked Jean, coming back into the room.

'Shall I tell her, or do you want to Betty?' asked Peggy.

Jean looked confused. 'Tell me what?'

Peggy didn't wait for Betty to reply. 'Betty's offered to help you in the shop. Isn't that great?'

It took a few moments to sink in, then emotionally Jean said, 'Betty, I don't know what to say. Are you sure?'

Peggy interrupted. 'I've already asked her that. Of course, she's sure.'

Jean shook her head. 'Will you shut up Peggy and let Betty answer for herself.'

Betty smiled. 'I'm already looking forward to it Jean. It'll be great fun. Not that I've ever worked in a shop before, so you'll have to teach me everything.'

Peggy stood up and said triumphantly, 'Now you don't have to sell to Mr Gishi.'

Jean laughed. 'Goshi, Peggy; it's Goshi.'

On the way back to the cottage the two women stopped to sit on a wooden bench overlooking a high reed bed. 'How are you doing now?' asked Peggy.

Betty sighed. 'Oh you know, good days and bad days, but there's no point in dwelling on what happened in London. It's in the past now, and Zed is safe down here, that's the most important thing.'

Although Betty disguised it well Peggy always detected an underlying sadness and who could blame her. She had lost her daughter to drugs, her son to prison, and now she and Zed had been forced to leave their home. Peggy put her arm around her shoulders. 'You know you are amongst friends down here, don't you?' asked Peggy.

Betty smiled. 'Of course I do. You've all been wonderful.'

When they reached the cottage there was a familiar face waiting for them.

'Hello Smokey,' said Peggy. 'What are you doing here?'

He picked up his long ex-army greatcoat which was draped over the balance beam of the lock.

'I've just left Ben at the cottage so thought I'd come over and cadge a cuppa, but there was nobody at home.'

'I expect Tim's still working at Harry's,' replied Peggy, opening the front door.

Smokey sat down on the sofa. 'How's things Betty?'

'Fine', she replied. 'The boys have settled in well to their new school, although I suspect Zed finds it a little harder, he's not as outgoing as Dwain.'

'We have some news,' said Peggy, coming in from the kitchen with three mugs of tea.

Smokey grinned. 'So do I.'

Peggy laughed. 'Go on then, you first.'

'I'm going to keep the cottage in Coote's Wood,' he said.

Peggy clapped her hands. 'Oh, I am so pleased. What changed your mind?'

He chuckled. 'It was Driftwood's call. We spun a coin, heads we keep it, tails it goes. Heads it was.'

Betty said, 'I think you have both made the right decision and he will always be there with you in spirit.'

He nodded. 'Yeah, at least I won't have to listen to the old devil snoring every night.'
Both women laughed at his banter, but it did little to disguise his grief.

'Any way what's your news?' he said, perking up.
'Betty's going to work with Jean in the shop,' said Peggy.

'I didn't know you had any shop experience,' replied Smokey.
Betty laughed. 'I don't. I'm just glad that Jean hasn't got one of those computerised tills.'

'She's saved the day. Jean was thinking of selling the shop,' said Peggy.

'What?' exclaimed Smokey, surprised.
Peggy then told him about the sleeping tablets. Smokey was shocked.

'Blimey! I didn't realise it was that bad.'
Betty added. 'Poor thing, she's absolutely exhausted.'

The rumbling noise from outside was unmistakable as Tim arrived back in his old Series One Land Rover. 'Listen to it,' said Peggy. 'It sounds just like an old tank.'
It was a few minutes, after parking at the rear of the cottage, before Tim came through the door.

'What's this? A conference?' he asked, stripping off his oily overalls and removing the steel toe capped boots.

Peggy chuckled. 'We were just trying to work out where you kept your money.'
Slumping down on the sofa next to Smokey, Tim said, 'Well let me know if you find any.' He sighed. 'I'm knackered mate, time I retired.'
Smokey laughed. 'You would be dead in a week.'

'We have some exciting news,' said Peggy. Tim groaned. 'Not more canal side gossip.'

Since the incident on the school fields with Tommy Hitch, Zed and Dwain were now very much part of the 'in' crowd, although unlike Dwain, Zed was cautious as to how far 'in' he became. On the bus to and from school Dwain now sat at the back with Phoebe and her boisterous friends. Zed on the other hand preferred the quiet company of her brother George and his friend Eddie. Though their backgrounds and upbringing could not have been more different their characters, interests were remarkably similar.

The school bus journey from Melbury Academy to Tiddledurn took roughly thirty minutes, depending on the traffic. The sad bus driver always reminded Zed and Dwain of old Dewey, the lollipop man at their school in Rotherhithe, who everyone always took the micky out of. As the coach slid alongside the kerb outside the newsagents in Tiddledurn, he would open the automatic doors, switch on the intercom, and deliver the same predictable announcement. *'Wakey wakey guys, it's home time'*. Then upping the volume. *'EVACUATE – EVACUATE,'* as if the coach were about to explode at any minute. This was always met by the youngsters with a collective groan, though some did often shout more colourful comments. But like Dewey no amount of insults seemed to penetrate his thick skin.

Disembarking onto the pavement the throng of tired youngsters quickly broke into small segments before heading off towards their homes. Seeing her mother, Lady Barrington Gore, waiting in her green Range Rover, Phoebe brushed her hand across Dwain's as she walked off.

She called to her brother George who was still talking to Zed and Eddie.

'See you,' he said, bumping fists with them. Turning to go, his blue eyes flashed across Zed's freckled face. He smiled. Though fleeting, it completely disarmed Zed. He blushed noticeably.

Poleaxed by the intensity of the moment and hoping that Eddie wasn't watching he quickly laughed it off. 'He's a cool dude.'

Eddie nodded. 'He's sound, man.'

Zed was unusually quiet as they both walked home across the village green.

Dwain nudged him. 'You alright, man?'

'Yeah, just thinking.'

'About what?' asked Dwain. Then laughing he said. 'You think too much, you'll fry yer brain.'

Zed did not reply. The thoughts consuming his mind were too personal and confusing to reveal.

With the recent letter from his uncle Darren and its implications, there were now two secrets he could not share, even with his best friend.

Smokey stayed to dinner that evening which pleased Zed and Dwain as, whenever they were together, he regaled them with stories from his army days and his and Driftwood's travels as men of the road. Tim would often raise an eyebrow and shake his head as fact and fiction merged. Not that the boys cared, Smokey could do no wrong in their eyes. He was a free spirit, something they both aspired to be.

Betty's steak and kidney pudding, made as she pointed out from her mother's recipe, went down a treat with the boys complaining that there were no second helpings. They were not disappointed though when Peggy produced her home-made apple pie with cream.

Tim rubbed his full belly. 'Blimey, that was good. Are you two in competition?'

After the boys had finished washing up Tim called them over to where he and Smokey were sitting on the sofa. 'I have a job for you.'

Warily Zed asked, 'What sort of job?'

Tim thoughtfully twisted the end of his droopy moustache. 'I want you to take Odin and Thor up to Boswell's Yard for blacking,' he said.

There was a look of confusion. 'What, with you and Peggy?' asked Dwain.

Tim shook his head. 'No, I'm too busy and Peg won't leave Betty.'

'What? On our own?' asked Zed.

Tim nodded. 'That's what I am saying.' He drank a mouthful of tea from his oversized mug. 'But then if you're not up to it?'

'No, no, course we are,' shouted Zed, nudging Dwain, who did not seem quite so enthusiastic at the prospect, but added cautiously, 'Yeah, it'll be cool.'

Smokey laughed. 'Look at them both. They're like rabbits caught in the headlights.'

Tim stood up. 'Right, that's it then, time and tide.'

Dwain chuckled. 'Waits for no man'.

'When do we go?' asked Zed.

'It's booked in for next week when you're on half term, so you will have plenty of time.'

Tim and Smokey went out into the garden. Betty was snoozing in the armchair by the fireplace.

'Well, you didn't expect that did you?' asked Peggy.

Zed shook his head. 'I still can't believe he's trusting us to take the boats on our own.'

Dwain laughed. 'I'm not sure I trust myself.'

'You'll be fine,' said Peggy. 'Just, remember everything we've taught you.'

The chirping chuckle of the cuckoo clock on the wall always caught Betty by surprise.

'Oh dear, is that the time? I must be going.'

Peggy was about to offer to walk her back across the green when Smokey came in from the garden and gallantly offered his services. 'Allow me to escort you Madam. There are highwaymen and braggards on the roads this time of night.' Betty laughed.

# CHAPTER NINE

## Kidnap

The following day after his return from London, Rocket Ron sat at the small round table in Rose's narrowboat moored near Muckle Farm. After experiencing the tsunami of people and heaving traffic in the great smoke he was happy to be back in this tranquil canal side location. Whilst Rose boiled up another batch of herbs, he removed the photocopies of the Melbury Echo from a buff envelope and laid them onto the wooden surface. From his coat pocket he took the red exercise book filled with the notes he had gleaned from the computer at the National Archive's in Kew and put it next to them.

Rose removed the bitter smelling herbs from the heat to cool and sat down beside him.

'So, what did you discover?' she asked eagerly. Ron opened the exercise book at the first page. 'It's most interesting. I'm sure there's more to the disappearance of Daisy Kearns than meets the eye.'

'But surely the police would have examined all this at the time?' asked Rose.
Ron gave a wry, conspiratorial smile. 'Maybe they chose not to. We need to divide up the timelines and facts of this case,' he said, turning to a blank page at the back of the book. He took a pencil then drew three evenly spaced horizontal lines.

Rose chuckled. 'You're beginning to sound like a detective.'

He laughed. 'The Rocket Ron Detective Agency, at your service.'

She shook her head. 'You silly old fool.'

Above the top line he wrote in capital letters.
DISAPPEARANCE FROM VILLAGE.
Underneath. 'DK BACKGROUND AND SERVICE
And below. OPERATION GREEN FIELDS.

'What's that?' asked Rose pointing to the third heading.

He shook his head. 'I don't know. I couldn't access the information. The files were marked classified. But I'm sure there's a link somewhere. If not, why was it on the computer documented amongst her files?'

'Sounds quite hush, hush,' observed Rose.
Ron nodded. 'Exactly. So, was she involved in some secret operation?'

Rose laughed. 'What! In sleepy Tiddledurn?'

'I don't know,' said Ron. 'That's what we need to find out.'

Bored with the proceedings Frankie and Freddie, his two ferrets, had curled up in a ball together on the carpet. 'Look at that,' said Rose, 'they're fast asleep.'
Ron laughed. 'It's those thick cuts of ham you feed them. They're not used to such luxuries.'

He tapped his finger on the newspaper photocopy of April 21st, 1943. 'We know she left the Royal Oak pub at 10.15 on the 14th of April. So, why did she leave on her own, and not with the other Land Army girls? Was it to make a phone call, and if so to whom?'

Rose asked. 'Why do you say that?' He pointed to the headlines in the Melbury Echo 28th April,
published one week later. 'Look here, a witness claims to have seen her by the phone box.'

'Could have been calling anybody, her parents or friends, maybe.'
He shrugged 'Doubt it, not at ten fifteen at night.'

'So, what did you find out about her at Kew?' asked Rose.

Ron pushed aside the newspaper copies and turned to his exercise book.

'Well,' he replied, running his finger across a line of his notes. 'The documents showed she came from Chislehurst in Kent. There must have been plenty of money as her father was Andrew Kearns of Kearns Paper Mills, and she was privately educated. She joined the ATS in August 1940 and was posted to a radar monitoring and development facility in Halstead, which is also in Kent. This is where she remained until September 1941. Now here's the thing,' he said, holding up the book, 'between October 1941 and February 1942, she disappears. There is no record of her service at all.'

Rose scratched her head. 'I need a cup of tea.' Ron agreed. 'Good idea. It's hard work being a detective.'

After a few minutes Rose put two mugs of tea and a plate of biscuits on the table.

'So, Sherlock, what have you deduced from all this?'

He smiled. 'Well, my dear Watson, where did she go between October 1941 and February 1942? And why would an obviously intelligent woman working at a radar monitoring and development site, transfer to the Land Army in March 1942 to milk cows and pick potatoes in Tidledurn?'

'Where do we go with this now then?' asked Rose.

'I think I need to visit the editor of the Melbury Echo again and see if she can help us.'

The boat suddenly rocked violently as a speeding vessel passed by.

Ron shot outside like a greyhound, which surprised Rose with his arthritic knees.

'Slow down, you stupid twat,' he shouted to the oblivious steerer, talking on his mobile phone. There was no response as wash from the boat crashed against the bank.

'It's getting worse, they've no consideration,' said Rose, when he returned.
He shook his head. 'The type of people using the waterways is certainly changing, and not always for the better.'

The commotion woke Freddie and Frankie who stood swaying groggily on the carpet. Rose lifted a jar from the shelf took out some doggy nibbles and scattered them around the boat.

'That'll keep them busy for a few minutes,' she laughed.

'You spoil 'em,' said Ron.
She chuckled. 'They're ferrets Ron, not children.'

To Bradley Seaton, Ryan Sharp, and Ashley Green, the men accused of setting fire to Betty's flat, the day had started like any other. As usual they met on the grass outside the housing estate at eleven o'clock. They rarely surfaced any earlier. In their line of work there was no requirement to do so. After a short walk along the busy Rotherhithe Road, they crossed over into Nickle Street.

Here, like every other morning, they entered Sid's greasy spoon café situated between a second-hand furniture shop and a chemist with metal security grills across the windows. Inside they sat at a table covered with lime green plastic tablecloths and ordered coffee and bacon rolls. At adjoining places, contemplating the emptiness of their lives, a few elderly people stared forlornly into mugs of milky tea.   Seaton sniffed loudly and checked his phone. Despite being on bail and wearing electronic tags their lucrative business activities would be unchanged, at least until they were banged up.

At ten minutes past midday, a moped bearing learner plates pulled up outside Sid's. The rider dismounted andentered the café without removing his helmet. Nobody, including Sid, seemed to notice or care. Unzipping his leather jacket, he pulled out a package and laid it on the table in front of the three men. No words were spoken during this transaction. Seaton nodded, took an envelope from his trouser pocket and handed it to the rider who placed it inside his jacket and left.

Seaton carefully opened the sealed package and examined it. He smiled. 'Good stuff.'
Then placing three small clear plastic bags on the table he divided the content into each. Sid came over with more bacon rolls, which like the previous ones were drowned in ketchup before being consumed. Seaton handed him some money, which wasn't payment for the food.

The green Audi turned from Rotherhithe Road into Nickle Street and parked. The previous day the passenger had received the message from Don Burns in Camp Hill Prison. 'Say hello to Horace.' A white transit van overtook the car and stopped outside the second-hand furniture store. Three heavies dressed in builders' overalls stepped from the rear of the van and went into Sid's café.  They ordered teas at the counter then sat at a table near to Seaton, Green, and Sharp.

Sid, not noted for his observational skills, had retreated to a safe distance. Seaton checked his phone. 'We need to go soon.' Each of them took one plastic bag off the table and dropped it into their pockets. Their daily routine would have been the same.

Following text requests for supplies, they would split up and traverse South London by public transport delivering the illegal product to their 'customers'.

When Ashley Green went to the counter to settle the bill, one of the watching heavies made a call on his mobile to the driver of the van who opened the rear doors and stood alongside on the pavement. Seaton and Sharp were already on their feet when Green returned.

Seaton sniffed. 'Let's go. We'll meet back 'ere tonight.' He pushed open the glass front door. Seaton was now outside on the pavement, the other two just behind him.

Then with the speed of leopards falling upon an Impala, the unsuspecting men were seized from behind and forced to the floor by the three heavies. Physically there was no contest, and such was the shock there was little time to shout out. With military precision the driver from the transit ran forward with cable ties and hoods. Then in a flash Seaton, Green and Sharp were being thrown like bags of rubbish into the back of the van. The doors slammed shut and the tyres screeched as it sped away from Nickle Street.

The green Audi pulled up outside the café and the three heavies in their builders' overalls got into the rear seats. As the car turned out onto the Rotherhithe Road the North London passenger made a call on his mobile phone.

Inside the café Sid gave his elderly customers a free mug of tea each saying, 'You didn't see anything, right?' They dutifully nodded.

That night on Turtle Zed could not sleep. He tossed and turned for some time before carefully unzipping his sleeping bag and stepping from the bed. Dwain who was sleeping next to him stirred but did not wake up.

Pulling on his tracksuit he went through the saloon and out onto the bow end of the boat. Either side was a bench seat. Breathing in the crisp and scented air he sat down on one and rested his feet on the gunwales. Occasionally an owl hooted in the distance or a vixen called, otherwise nothing penetrated the thick wall of silence which surrounded him.

Closing his eyes, he felt the sheer intensity of the darkness within and without, safe and secure as if wrapped in the swirls of a wizard's inky cloak. High above, tropospheric shadows clouded the sickle half-moon's mesmerising aura. A lonely satellite scurried quickly by the constellations in its quest to orbit the earth. He wondered if like rainbows, there was a pot of gold where shooting stars fell. A badger snuffled slowly along the towpath before being swallowed by the gloom.

At the periphery of his vision a glimmer of watery grey light was seeping into the blackness, heralding the start of a new day. Like King Canute with the incoming tide, he wished he could hold the day back, at least until he had made sense of the events of the previous one. He jumped as Dwain, dressed only in his boxer shorts, suddenly appeared at the door beside him. He shivered. 'What are you doing out here dude? It's too early. And don't say you were thinking.'

Zed smiled. 'Alright then, I was meditating.'
Dwain shook his head. 'You're losing it man, I'm going back to bed.'

After he had gone Zed thought how wonderful it must be to have such an untroubled and uncomplicated mind as his friend.

He did not go back to bed. Instead lying on the sofa he turned on his phone and once again studied the message from his Uncle Darren. It was sent at ten past nine the previous evening and simply said. 'IT'S DONE'.

# CHAPTER TEN

## Willie Watkins

Smokey Joe looked around the inside of the aged caravan in the woods at Old Moor Lock. In between lengthy jaunts around the country as a man of the road it had been his home for several years now, a place to return to, a haven and refuge. Noticing himself in a cracked wall mounted mirror, he mused on how the tired and shabby interior of the caravan reflected his own dishevelled appearance. But then the caravan had only ever been meant as a base; like his old mate Driftwood, his real love had been the byways and highways of England.

His was never a conventional childhood. The nearest he ever got to experiencing parental normality was when, in the school holidays, he stayed with his aunt and uncle in Coote's Wood. Not that his parents were in anyway bad, just emotionally dysfunctional.

He put on his wide brimmed hat with freshly plucked pheasant feather and went outside. Sitting on the step overlooking the clearing, his mind drifted back to the warm summer evening in 2006 when he had first met Willie Watkins.

Smokey had returned home after serving in the Iraq war for three years. Not wishing to stay in Birmingham, the place of his birth, he had ended up in Melbury, or at least his body had. His mind like splintered shrapnel still lay scattered throughout several foreign conflicts. Initially he had intended staying with his aunt and uncle in the cottage at Coote's Wood near Tiddledurn, but an overwhelming desire to be alone with his demons drove him from that path. It was a decision he would always regret.

As the years rolled on and he became more reclusive. Kindling old relationships or creating new ones grew ever more difficult for him. Both his uncle and aunt had died not knowing how geographically and emotionally close to them he was believing that, like his parents in Birmingham, they had lost contact with him.

Smokey reached into his trouser pocket and pulled out the Swiss Army clasp knife which Willie Watkins had given him all those years ago. He always carried it even to this day. Willie had been the banksman at Old Moor Lock for many years. Everyone locally knew Willie. He was a small generous man with a big heart.

Smokey smiled as he remembered those past summer's evenings, when he had first camped in the woods at Old Mill Lock. Tired and hungry after leaving the train at Melbury, it was the first place he found along the towpath where he could off load the heavy rucksack and pitch his small tent. It was the smoke from the fire which he had lit to cook some tea which attracted the attention of Willie Watkins and his Jack Russell, Sarge, both of whom lived in the caravan which Smokey now occupied.

Willie was a pint-sized man with the best of his working years behind him. He had a kind weathered face with a curved Peterson pipe permanently clasped between his crooked nicotine-stained teeth. It would be the start of a lasting friendship, with Smokey regularly helping him with the often-heavy work maintaining the canal banks and towpaths. As the autumn of that first year retreated and winter tightened its grip,

Willie had suggested to Smokey that he might like to abandon his tent and move into the caravan with him and Sarge.

Sadly, a year later in gale force winds, a tall unstable and diseased silver birch, ended Willie's life prematurely. Sarge who had been scratching furiously at the caravan door led Smokey to a corner of the woods where Willie had been clearing undergrowth. Smokey rushed to comfort his trapped friend but there was little to be done.

After the funeral Smokey stayed on in the caravan, each day expecting someone to arrive and claim ownership, but no one ever did. Sarge, who was already in advanced years, pined daily for his old master. Eventually he stopped eating and died shortly afterwards. Smokey buried him at the edge of the clearing in the woods.

He got back up from the step and went inside the caravan. His dilemma now was what to do with his old home when he moved to Coote's Wood. He couldn't just leave it to rot, Willie would not have approved of that. On the shelf beside the window a red bowler hat and a plastic urn reminded him of his other dilemma, what to do with Driftwood's ashes.

The recent renovation of the cottage in Coote's Wood was going well. Ben, the carpenter, had finished replacing the wooden veranda and the builder was on target to complete the damaged roof. All Smokey had to do now was summon up the enthusiasm to move into it, and that would not be easy. Although with Driftwood's spiritual intervention his mind was made up, the thought of living in the cottage on his own troubled him. Like any competent enemy the demons knew his weaknesses and were always ready to strike.

The last day of school before the half term break, was as usual a raucous affair. Nobody was interested in learning, as a week's freedom beckoned. For most teenagers this would mean sleeping in late, then endless hours spent playing computer games or communicating with friends on social media. Unfortunately for Zed and Dwain they would not have the option of this sedentary style vacation.

The final bell heralded a mass exodus from every corner of the school. Those youngsters bound for Tiddledurn and its surrounding villages boarded the waiting school bus with its sad driver. As was usual Phoebe occupied the back seat with her girlfriends. Dwain of course was amongst them. Zed and George sat together further to the front. Eddie, their other friend, had stayed late at school for a five-a-side football match.

'So, what you doing at half term?' asked Zed. George shook his head. 'Not sure yet, you?' Zed told him about taking the boats, Odin and Thor, to Boswell's Yard for blacking. George was intrigued. He knew that Zed and Dwain had connections to the canal and narrowboats but hadn't realised they were competent enough to handle them on a journey.

'Wow,' he exclaimed. 'That sound brill, man.' Zed nodded nonchalantly. 'Yeah, it's great.' He thought for a moment. 'Why don't you and Phoebe come with us?'

'Really, are you serious?' exclaimed George, surprised by the sudden invitation. Zed shrugged. 'Why not, it'll be cool.'

As the bus approached Tiddledurn the irritating driver delivered his predictable message across the tannoy. 'Wakey, wakey guys! Home time. EVACUATE, EVACUATE.' There was the same collective groan from the captive teenage audience.

At first Phoebe was reluctant to share George's enthusiasm to Zed's offer. Her initial reaction being, 'Is it safe and does it have a shower?' George raised his eyebrows in disbelief.

'What Pheeb? Surely you can do without a shower for one week?'
She looked aghast at the thought. Dwain, sensing an opportunity, placed his arm around her shoulder.

'It'll be great Phoebe. You could have one of the skipper's cabins, there's a sink and hot water.' He laughed. 'And I promise no peeping.'

'We'll have to ask my mother first,' she replied, mellowing slightly. Sensing victory Dwain smiled.

There was the impatient honking of a car's horn as their mother, Lady Barrington Gore, pulled up in her green Range Rover. 'I'll text you later,' George called to Zed as he and Phoebe ran across the road to the waiting vehicle.

Over dinner that evening Tim's mood changed suddenly.

'How long have you known the Barrington Gores?' he asked abruptly.

'They're in our year at school,' Zed replied defensively, having previously mentioned that he had invited Phoebe and George to join them on the trip to Boswell's Yard.
Tim nodded thoughtfully then grumbled. 'Well, let's just hope they're better than previous generations.'

Zed and Dwain exchanged confused looks.

Zed's gran, Betty, not understanding Tim's irritation asked, 'How do you mean?'

Tim stood, picked his mug up from the table and walked towards the kitchen. 'It doesn't matter, it was a long time ago. Forget it.'

Peggy called after him. 'That's not fair Tim. George and Phoebe are their friends. You can't just leave them wondering what you meant.'

He turned, walked back across the room to the table and sat down. He hesitated for a moment as if locating the story from somewhere deep in his mind, then began.

'For centuries the Barrington Gores owned much of the land around here. Most of the farmers were their tenants.'

'What does that mean?' asked Dwain.

Peggy explained. 'They rented the land from the Barrington Gores.' Dwain nodded.

Tim continued. 'And that system worked well for generations, some farms doing better than others, but they always had a roof over their heads and food on the table. Then in 1937 Morris Barrington Gore died and his eldest son, Edgar, took over. Unlike his father he had little time for his tenants or their way of life.'

Peggy interrupted him. 'There was also a younger brother, Wilf.'

Tim gave a wry smile. 'Ah yes, we'll come to him later. Anyway, a year after taking over the estate Edgar raised the rents on some of the farms to an amount completely out of proportion to their annual income.'

He coughed loudly. Peggy suggested she made them all a cup of tea. The boys followed her into the kitchen to grab some cold juice. Tim asked Betty if she had been

informed of the trial date of the men who set fire to her flat. She shook her head. 'Nothing yet, although my neighbour Doris told me she hadn't seen them about the estate, which is strange as they're out on bail.
Tim exhaled in exasperation. 'Unbelievable, they should already be locked up.'

Peggy arrived back at the table with a plastic tray holding three mugs of tea. The boys had opted for blackcurrant flavoured ice pops.

Tim added two spoons of sugar to the strong brew and stirred it slowly in his oversized mug. Before he could speak Zed asked. 'So, what happened to the farmers and their families?'
Tim sighed. 'The inevitable. People couldn't afford the new rents so they were forced to give up the farms and move out. Those who tried to stay were eventually evicted.'
Peggy added. 'Sadly, Tim's Great Uncle Frank was amongst them.'
Tim nodded. 'Yes, his family who had farmed here for years was evicted.'

'Where did they go?' asked Dwain.

'They stayed here in this cottage for a while, then found a small house in Melbury. But it destroyed them and a year later he died. My father told me he just gave up.'

Betty asked, 'But why did this Edgar suddenly put up the rents, and only on certain farms?'

Tim replied. 'Nobody was quite sure at the time. But suspicions were aroused when it was realised that they were all in the same geographical area. Then all was revealed; he was selling the land to a property developer for housing.'

Betty said. 'So, all those lives were destroyed so he could get richer.'

Tim nodded. 'Exactly so. Pure greed.'

'So, what about Wilf, the brother?' asked Dwain.

Now Peggy continued the story. 'When he was twenty five, Wilf got involved with a village girl called Alice Cook. She was sixteen at the time.
Her parents, Albert and Mary ran the garage in the high street and obviously knew nothing about this relationship. Anyway, one thing led to another and she became pregnant.

'By him?' asked Betty.

Peggy smiled. 'Well of course he denied it, but nobody including her parents believed him. After all, she hadn't been with anybody else. Her father Albert was furious and threatened to kill him if he ever showed his face in the village again.

'Why did he deny it was him?' asked Zed.

Tim laughed contemptuously. 'Because he was a spoilt brat who, instead of taking responsibility for his actions, hid behind his brother Edgar in the Manor House.'

'What happened to the baby?' asked Betty.

Peggy said, 'Such was the shame on the family, that after the birth she was forced to give the child up for adoption.'

Zed was shocked. 'That's terrible. So, she never saw it anymore?'

Peggy shrugged. 'Who knows? But I doubt it.'

Betty said, 'They were different times Zed. It used to happen a lot in those days.'

Betty jumped as the cuckoo clock on the wall called nine. She laughed. 'That thing always catches me by surprise. Now I must be going, get my beauty sleep.'

'You can't go yet Gran. Tim hasn't finished the story.'

Tim stood up. 'Your gran's right. It's getting late. You'll have to wait until tomorrow evening for the next instalment.'

'I'll walk you back,' said Peggy. After helping Betty on with her coat, she took her own from the hook behind the door. Zed and Dwain kissed Betty goodnight.

Tim took a long black rubber torch from the sideboard drawer. 'Come on you two, I'll come back to Turtle with you, then I can check the mooring lines on Odin and Thor.'

Reluctantly Zed and Dwain lifted themselves from the comfortable sofa, put on their jackets and followed Tim outside into the dark chilly May evening.

# CHAPTER ELEVEN

## Morning Trek

It was a bright spring morning. Rocket Ron left his two
ferrets, Frankie and Freddie, with Rose on her boat,
then set out from his moorings at Muckle Farm along
the towpath towards Melbury. Due to his ever-
worsening arthritic knees the trek into town would
prove more challenging for him. With the aid of a stout,
self-carved walking stick he estimated that it should
take him just under two hours. He enjoyed sauntering
alongside the canal especially at this time of morning,
although parts of the towpath were badly maintained
and he often had to navigate wide puddles and an
uneven surface.

There were few boats moored along this stretch
of the canal, mainly because it was too shallow for them
to get alongside. Those who had needed a plank, or
brow, placed between the boat and the bank to get
ashore. A short distance further along, the towpath
ended abruptly. Ron crossed over the arched bridge to
the other side of the canal. There was a wooden bench
dedicated to a Leonard Kimmings 1940 – 2019, who
loved to fish this spot. Ron welcomed the opportunity
to sit down and rest his aching legs. Raising his eyes
skyward, he said loudly, 'Thanks Leonard.' He
imagined him in all weathers sitting peacefully on the
bank mesmerized by a small round float bobbing about
in the water. Ron never quite understood why people
did it, but he admired their tenacity.

He closed his eyes and let the silence wash over
him. Moments later his meditative peace was disturbed
by approaching voices.

As he opened his eyes, two people wearing wet suits and standing on brightly coloured paddle boards, emerged from behind a weeping willow. He estimated that they were both in their late twenties. The first to appear, a woman, seemed supremely confident, balancing effortlessly on the flat surface, the paddle in her hands hardly rippling the water. Her partner, a few feet behind, less so.

'How the devil do you stay upright?' called Ron.

The young man laughed. 'With difficulty mate. I've been off twice already.'

Ron watched them both disappear round the bend in the canal then stood up and stretched. It was only a short distance now to Tim's cottage. He decided to call in for a brew. Normally Tim or Peggy would be at home.

Soon the low hedgerows, which bordered the arable farm fields beyond, gave way to the dense, tangled trees of Coote's Wood. He passed the tall wooden gate which led onto the gravel track and the clearing beyond where Smokey Joe's cottage was being renovated. Drawing nearer to the lock side cottage he could hear the flow of water seeping from the bottom gates. The two swans, Sammy and Sheena, swam nearby with their four recently hatched cygnets following their parents closely.

Climbing up the small grass mound at the side of the lock, Ron crossed over using the narrow walkway attached to the gates. It seemed strange walking across the lawn without Barney, Tim's collie, running to greet him. He looked with sadness at the small grave underneath the apple tree, the inscribed wooden heart indicating Barney's final resting place.

Before reaching the front door, he heard classical music coming from the side of the building. A year ago Tim had bought Peggy a shepherd's hut so she had space to pursue her love of canal art. Zed and Dwain laughingly called it a shed on wheels. Ron walked to the far end of the white painted cottage. The four wheeled wooden structure was parked near to Tim's workshop. The door was open. He climbed up the four wooden steps and banged on the side. 'Anyone at home?'

Wearing a green, paint splattered smock Peggy was sitting on a swivel chair painting a yellow rose onto a brown china teapot. Above her was a shelf full of finished items, most of which would be sold in Jean's canal side shop. Startled, she turned.

'Oh Ron, I didn't see you.'
He smiled. 'You were concentrating. Sorry to disturb.'

'Not at all, I could do with a break. My eyes are not as young as they used to be.' She put down her paint brush, switched off the radio and swung around on the chair. 'How about a nice cup of tea.'

Inside the cottage Ron sank into the sofa's deep cushions. He looked around the comfortable and tidy room. 'You've certainly made this place look homely,' he said.

Peggy called from the kitchen. 'Yes, Tim did lead a rather drab, spartan existence.'
Ron chuckled to himself when he thought of his own frugal lifestyle on his boat. Peggy placed two mugs of tea and a homemade fruit cake on the coffee table. Outside there was the unmistakable thud of the lock gates closing, followed by the sound of gushing water as someone flooded the chamber.

'That's the first boat through today,' said Peggy.

Ron checked his watch and chuckled. 'It's still early. Most of the hire boat people will be in bed.'

Peggy sat opposite and handed him a piece of cake. 'So where are you off too?'

He told her about the call yesterday from Sharon Giddings, the editor of the Melbury Echo regarding the disappearance of the Land Army girl, Daisy Kearns. The phone call had taken him by surprise, as the last time they met she indicated there was little else she could do to help him.

Peggy smiled. 'Tim told me you were looking into that. It was a long time ago now.'

Ron nodded. 'It's always bugged me. Every time I walk around Muckle Farm, I wonder what happened to that poor girl. It's almost as if her spirit is calling to me. I'm sure there's more to it than meets the eye.'

Their conversation was abruptly interrupted by loud panicked shouting from outside. Both Ron and Peggy jumped up and made for the door. The double lock was opposite the cottage at the far side of the lawn. A woman, who moments earlier had opened the side paddles to empty the full chamber, now watched horrified and helpless as the bow of their boat tilted down at a frightening angle, leaving the stern end elevated. Equally mortified, the stressed male steerer was waving his arms and shouting to the woman, who couldn't hear him above the noise of the engine.

Peggy and Ron, both seasoned boaters, instantly recognised the dilemma. The sixty foot narrowboat had been positioned too far back in the lock. As the water under the hull had drained away, the stern end had been caught on the concrete cill.

Peggy quickly ran towards the frozen woman and grabbed the windlass from her hand. Taking the tension off the ratchet she lifted the safety catch or pawl, removed the windlass from the spindle and let the paddle drop. Crossing over the gates, she did the same on the other side.

Anticipating her move, Ron had taken a windlass from the steerer, raised the paddles on the top gates and re-flooded the chamber. As the water level rose rapidly the boat lifted, lurched one way then another before finally settling in the agitated water. Leaning shakily against the balance beam the frozen faced woman thawed slightly.

'Thank the Lord you were here,' she said to Peggy.

Peggy nodded. 'That was a close thing my dear, but I don't think God was much help.'

The woman laughed. Ron was standing at the side of the lock talking to the now calm steerer.

'Do you think it's damaged?' he asked.

Ron shrugged. 'Difficult to tell, you weren't on the cill for very long.'

Regaining her composure, the woman told Peggy that they had only bought the boat two weeks ago. She grimaced. 'I'm afraid we are complete novices.'

Peggy laughed sympathetically, 'We were all novices once, dear.'

She and Ron stayed there long enough to see them through the lock. They waved as the pair exited the bottom gates. 'Looks like they've got away without any damage,' Ron said.

Peggy agreed, 'It's worrying though, isn't it?'

It was gone eleven when Ron departed the cottage to resume his walk into Melbury Town.

Had Tim been at home he would have given him a lift in the Land Rover, but he had left much earlier for Harry Martin's marina, taking Zed and Dwain with him to help with a job on one of the hire boats. Ambling slowly along the towpath Ron he wondered in excited anticipation what further information the editor Sharon Giddings may have unearthed. He needed a breakthrough if he was to make any headway soon with the disappearance of Daisy Kearns.

The offices of the Melbury Echo occupied an old branch of the former town bank. The red brick, two storey building stood on the corner of the High Street and Millfield Road. One of the larger front windows displayed black and white pictures of recently covered events in and around the town. Ron pushed open the glass door and walked into the colourfully decorated reception area.

The receptionist, a young woman with short mousy hair, sat behind a polished counter. Ron noticed a coloured tattoo of a butterfly on her right forearm.

She smiled at him. 'It means, Beauty, Transformation and Freedom.
Ron nodded, 'Is that right? I'll have to get one then.'
She giggled.

'I'm here to see Sharon Giddings,' he said.

She indicated to a red, bench sofa. 'Take a seat over there, and I'll let her know you are here.'

He was glad to sit down and rest his weary, aching legs. The walk into town had proved a little too ambitious. After the meeting he would take a taxi back to Muckle Farm. He had just picked up a magazine from the coffee table when Sharon Giddings came bustling through a connecting door. She was an impressive woman, large in build with shoulder length red hair. Ron was sure it was blue last time they met. Her cream-coloured spectacles seemed to take up the whole of her face.

'Hello Ron,' she gushed, holding out her hand for him to shake. 'Good to see you again. Come on through. I think I may have something of interest for you.'

Ron smiled and followed her through the door. As he sat down in her office, he did wonder how such an obviously efficient woman could operate in such chaos. Each of the four surrounding chairs was piled high with back copies of the newspaper. The surface of her large desk was hidden beneath stacks of files and an assortment of loose documents. A young man wearing a red T shirt with 'Zombies Eat Brains' printed on it, came into the office with two cups of tea and some biscuits.

Sharon Giddings sat down behind the cluttered desk. She peered at him through her impressive glasses. 'Well Ron, I was intrigued after your last visit, so I tasked one of our reporters to investigate further the Daisy Kearns case. She extracted a pink wallet folder from the stack beside her computer, then handed it to Ron. She chuckled loudly. 'Before you read the content, I have to inform you that some of the information was obtained clandestinely.'

Intrigued, Ron opened the folder and took out the enclosed papers.

# CHAPTER TWELVE

## The Story

Over dinner at the cottage the following evening, Zed's gran opened her handbag and produced a letter which had arrived in the post that morning. She pulled the crisp white sheet from the buff official-looking envelope then announced.

'It's from the Crown Prosecution Service in London, saying that the trial has been postponed indefinitely as the three defendants are medically unfit to enter a plea.'

Tim laughed. 'Defendants, is that what they call them? Scumbags more like. And how the devil did all three become incapacitated at the same time?'

Betty shrugged. 'Maybe they've all been in a car accident together.'

Peggy said, 'It all sounds a bit dodgy to me.'

Zed said nothing. He did not know exactly what had happened to Bradley Seaton, Ryan Sharp and Ashley Green, but he remembered his Uncle Darren's chilling text message to him. 'It's done.'

The boys though were more interested in hearing the continuation of Tim's story about the dark past of Phoebe and George's family, the Barrington Gores. Aware of their eager anticipation, Tim mischievously teased them by taking longer to finish his dinner. After the last piece of Cumberland sausage had left his fork he wiped his mouth slowly with a cloth napkin. 'Beautiful. My compliments to the chef.' He turned towards the two boys. 'Now, how about a nice brew?'

Zed and Dwain groaned at the deliberate delaying tactics but reluctantly went into the kitchen to make the tea.

Peggy shook her head. 'You do wind them up.' He smiled. The boys returned with Tim's oversized mug and two smaller cups.

Peggy said to Tim, 'Now, will you put them out of their misery.'

Betty laughed. 'And me.'
Tim took a long gulp of tea then said, 'Not a bad brew. Now where was I?'

'You were telling us about Wilf,' said Zed eagerly.
Tim nodded. 'Ah yes. As well as Albert's very real threat to kill Wilf, his brother Edgar was also in fear of reprisals from angry former tenants, so neither moved very far from the relative safety of the Manor House. However, whilst Edgar was occasionally spotted out and about, Wilf was never seen. Then rumours started to surface in the village that he had been squirreled away out of the country.

'Where did he go?' asked Dwain.
Tim took another mouthful of tea. 'Nobody knew, though some time later and by pure chance all was revealed.' Zed and Dwain could hardly contain their curiosity. Peggy and Betty had never seen them so quiet. Tim smiled to himself, remembering how as a young boy his grandfather had told him the story, at this very table.

He continued. 'One March night in 1939 there was a devil of a storm; lightening, loud crashes of thunder and rain the size of marbles.

A lightweight plane heading for a small airfield near Melbury was forced to crash land in a cabbage field near Haddon village. The farmer, who had heard the plane skim over his roof and fearing the worst, called the emergency services.

'Was anyone killed?' asked Zed, hoping for some gory details.

Tim shook his head. 'No, there was only the pilot on board and he managed to land it, albeit nose down in the muddy field. Unfortunately for him the cabin door jammed, and he couldn't escape.'

'He was lucky it didn't catch fire and explode,' said Dwain.

Tim agreed. 'He was fortunate not to have a full tank of fuel. Anyway, when the fire brigade arrived they quickly forced open the door to free him.' He chuckled loudly. 'Then to their astonishment, instead of thanking them, he ran off into the surrounding woods.'

'Didn't they go after him?' asked Zed.

Tim shrugged. 'Why would they? They were local volunteer firemen and it was also pitch dark. When the police turned up, they searched the plane and found it filled with contraband.'

Before the boys could ask, Peggy said, 'That's goods that have been imported illegally.'

Betty added, 'Smuggled, like pirates of old.'

'That's right,' said Tim, 'and apparently he had been doing it for some time, right under the nose of the authorities.'

Dwain asked. 'So, did they catch him?'

Tim smiled. 'Oh yes. They found him hiding in the attic of his house in Melbury.'

Suddenly the cuckoo in the wall clock roused itself to noisily announce the twentieth hour.

As usual Betty jumped as it caught her by surprise. 'Is that the time? I must be going in an hour.'

Anticipating her next sentence being, 'I must get my beauty sleep,' Zed said, 'You're already beautiful Gran.'

She laughed. 'Well thank you Zed. What a compliment!'

Dwain, looking slightly bewildered, asked, 'But what's all this got to do with Wilf?'

Tim held up his forefinger. 'Patience, patience.' He paused. 'Now, you remember I said Wilf's whereabouts were revealed by chance.' The boys nodded attentively. Tim coughed, always a sign that another brew would be required soon. 'After being arrested, the pilot was taken to Melbury Police Station for questioning. At first, he was reluctant to say much about his recent clandestine activities. But the threat of a long prison sentence seemed to loosen his tongue. He could hardly claim innocence after being caught red handed. It was during this interrogation that he revealed how some weeks earlier he had been paid to fly someone out of the country. At first, he wouldn't say who the passenger was, but eventually admitted the man had been Wilf Barrington Gore, who he had flown to Munich in Germany.'

'But why Germany?' asked Zed. 'France is nearer.' Then he hesitated. 'Isn't it?'

Tim smiled. 'It is Zed, but apparently they had cousins living in Munich. Many years beforehand, Wilf and Edgar's grandfather had married Freda Von Westerhugan, the daughter of a German aristocratic family.'

Betty asked, 'They're half German then?'

Tim nodded. 'It would seem so.' He chuckled. 'A bit like our Royals.'

'Did Wilf ever come back to England?' asked Dwain.

Tim stretched then yawned. 'He did, but that's a story for another day.'

That night on board Turtle, as darkness nudged against the curtained windows and rain danced rhythmically on the roof, Dwain and Zed lay talking late into the night. They were still trying to digest Tim's story and whether George and Phoebe knew of the family's heavy baggage. Dressed in T shirts and track suit bottoms they relaxed into the deep folds of their sleeping bags.

As rippling water lapped against the boat's hull, the warm glow of the bedside lamp enhanced the cosiness of the small stern cabin. Then Dwain turned to Zed and asked directly. 'Do you fancy George?'

Taken by surprise, Zed felt the heat rising in his cheeks. His voice clamped tight inside his throat. Tears started to fill his eyes.

Dwain said gently, 'It's cool man, really.'

Zed lay still, staring at the roof, thin wisps of water running down his freckled face. 'How did you know?' he asked softly.

Dwain smiled, 'It's the way you look at him.'

Zed said, 'I didn't understand it at first. It just happened.' He started to sob. 'Now you think I'm a gay weirdo.'

Dwain leant across, put his arm around Zed then kissed him on the forehead. 'I don't care what you are. You're my bruv and I luv yer.' He laughed. 'Now we better get some kip, or Tim will be banging on the boat in the morning.' Zed turned off the bedside lamp. Dwain soon succumbed to tiredness.

Zed stayed awake a little longer, his young, confused mind processing the enormity of the last few moments. Then he felt a sudden relief.

The veil of darkness which had engulfed Turtle lifted slowly, creating the illusion that the morning hour was earlier than supposed. Persistent heavy rain which had fallen throughout the night now tapered off into a buffeting drizzle. Dwain woke first, fumbled blindly for his phone, and switched it on. Seconds later the screen illuminated projecting a small beam of light into the inky cabin. The time shown was eight forty five. He swore under his breath, punched Zed hard on his shoulder then jumped from the bed.

Zed slowly opened his eyes. 'What?' he mumbled groggily.

Struggling to get his jeans on, Dwain shouted, 'We're supposed to meet Tim at the cottage at eight thirty.'

Zed groaned loudly and slid from the bed. He yawned. 'What time is it?'

Dwain threw a sweaty T shirt at him. 'Late. Get dressed and hurry up.'

After throwing on their coats they left the boat and ran along the slippery towpath towards the cottage. Peggy looked aghast as the dishevelled, soggy pair burst through the front door. She held up her hands and shouted. 'Stop right there.' The boys halted abruptly as if turned to stone.

'You are not sitting down to breakfast in that state. Have you washed this morning?'

Sheepishly both boys shook their heads.

Peggy pointed at Zed. 'And your hair looks as tangled as a sheep's backside.' Dwain chuckled. He escaped such criticism as his black frizzy hair was cut short. Hearing Peggy's shout Tim came in from his workshop behind the cottage.

'Oh, they've surfaced at last, have they?' he asked sarcastically.

Dwain said, 'Sorry Tim, we overslept.'

He laughed. 'I can see that.'

Peggy wasn't finished with them yet. 'Are they the same T shirts you were wearing yesterday?'

They both nodded sullenly.

'Late and smelly,' Tim said, flopping down onto the sofa.

Having voiced her displeasure Peggy mellowed. 'Right, take those wet coats and shoes off and sit down at the table.'

They looked at Tim for his approval. He chuckled. 'Go on, we can go to Harry's later.'

They hungrily ate cornflakes as the smell of frying bacon wafted in from the kitchen.

Tim asked, 'Have you heard anymore from your friends about going on the boats with you?'

'Not yet,' Dwain replied.

Tim nodded thoughtfully.

Zed scooped up the last of the milk from his bowl. 'Are you going to tell us more about Wilf later?'

Tim stroked his droopy moustache and stretched. 'Well, that depends on whether you can stay awake after dinner.'

They both groaned and grinned at each other.

Peggy put two fried breakfasts on the table then said, 'When you've eaten that you can go back to the boat, shower and put some clean clothes on.'

With mouthfuls of food, they both nodded.

Tim shook his head. 'Teenagers!'

Outside the cottage the blustery chilled drizzle had abated, heightening warm rays of early summer sun as they washed softly across the façade of the weathered building. Tim looked out through the sash window to the lawn beyond. A fulsome, wispy bush tapped gently on the glass pane.

Tim eased himself up from the sofa then stretched to relieve his aching back. 'Right! Time and tide….. Looks a bit better out there now.'

'What were you doing in the workshop?' enquired Zed.

Tim emitted a disgruntled sigh. 'Well, in the absence of my unclean apprentices, this morning I decided to sharpen the blades on the mower.'

Zed wished he hadn't asked. Both boys stood up, took their empty plates from the table and went towards the kitchen.

Peggy said, 'I'll take those, you go back and clean yourselves up.'

As they went out through the front door Tim called, 'Don't take all day.'

Walking quickly back along the towpath towards Turtle Zed suddenly stopped. 'You won't tell anyone about last night, will you?'

'How do you mean?' Dwain asked.

Zed paused then said quietly, 'About me and George.'

Dwain punched him playfully on the arm. 'Cos not dude. Now come on or we'll get more grief from Tim and Peggy.'

# CHAPTER THIRTEEN

## Missing

Jackdaw, a sixty foot narrowboat with eight berths, was the first and oldest vessel in Harry Martin's hire fleet of ten boats. Over the years it had more than earned its cost price many times over. But now the old workhorse needed a new engine which Tim, along with his two 'apprentices' Zed and Dwain, was due to fit. However, before doing that they would need to lift out the old one; no mean feat. For Zed and Dwain it would be another valuable and practical experience in Marine Engineering, something they had both decided to do after leaving school.

When the boys hurriedly arrived back at the cottage Tim had already loaded the rear of the Land Rover with the tools and equipment he needed to remove the heavy engine from Jackdaw.

'We're back,' called Zed, as he and Dwain walked around the side of the cottage. Tim closed and locked the workshop door before acknowledging them. 'Well, you two certainly look cleaner than earlier.'

A voice from behind them added, 'And smell a lot fresher.' Peggy handed them a large carrier bag containing three packed lunches and two pairs of clean overalls. She had given up asking Tim if he wanted his washed. They were only being held together by oil and grease.

'Right. Time and tide.....' said Tim, opening the Land Rover door and jumping into the driver's seat. Zed and Dwain climbed up next to him.

'Have a good day,' called Peggy, as they pulled away noisily from the cottage. The boys waved. Tim tooted the horn.

She shook her head. 'It still sounds like an old tank.'

The old series one Land Rover wasn't built for comfort. Zed and Dwain bounced about on the hard front seat as Tim crashed through the gears on their way to Harry Martin's marina. It was as they entered the roundabout on the other side of Tiddledurn that Zed and Dwain's mobile phones pinged. They both pulled them from their pockets and studied the screens. It was a text message from George and Pheobe. 'Sorry can't cum on boat trip, laters.'

Zed and Dwain exchanged a disappointed glance. After a few moments of moody silence Tim asked, 'What's up then?'

Zed replied sullenly. 'Phoebe and George can't go on the trip to Boswell's Yard.'

Tim engaged fourth gear as the speedometer flickered at fifty miles per hour.

'Did they say why?' he asked.

Both boys shook their heads. Unbeknown to them, Tim was breathing a sigh of relief. Since it had been suggested, he and Peggy had been uneasy about the idea, though they didn't want to upset the boys.

Dwain said, 'It would have been easier with four of us.'

Tim nodded, on that point he agreed with him.

They turned off the main road onto a narrow lane which led to the marina entrance. Overhanging trees brushed along the canvas roof and the water from potholes, flooded with last night's rain, splashed against the sides. Tim complained. 'Makes you wonder why we pay road tax.'

Harry was standing on the service pontoon talking to Roy Coombs, the new owner of the narrowboat, Noggin. A quiet, affable character in his late sixties, he had always fancied a life afloat on the inland waterways, so after retiring from the City of London where he had spent most of his working life, he set out to find a boat. After many months of searching around the country he found the ideal vessel, a fifty five foot trad stern. It was a private sale from a young couple moored on a permanent towpath mooring near to Melbury Lock.

With little knowledge of boats and needing to gain experience he decided to moor the boat in Harry Martin's marina. From here he could make small trips on the canal whilst improving his handling skills. Harry liked him and they often spoke briefly discussing the normal casual topics, which of course included the weather. Not that any interaction with Harry was ever brief as everything was repeated twice. As Roy walked away towards his boat on the far side of the marina Harry was struck by how happy he seemed with his new way of life.

Harry waved as Tim pulled up in the Land Rover. 'Kettle's on, I say kettle's on,' he called out as Tim stepped from the driver's seat. The boys tumbled out of the opposite side.

Zed asked, 'How you doing Harry?'
He shrugged. 'Staying afloat, just. I say, just.'
Tim chuckled as he looked at Harry's new Volvo parked beside the office. He had been claiming to be 'just keeping afloat' for years.

Inside the office they sat around Harry's cluttered desk while he busied himself in the adjoining kitchen. Zed texted George. 'Y U NOT CUM.' Dwain sent a similar one to Phoebe.

Tim watched as their thumbs moved quickly across the screens. He guessed who they were messaging. Harry pushed aside a pile of papers and put two mugs of tea and some biscuits on the desk. Tim joked about the chocolate digestives not lasting long.

The office door was open and a cool breeze blew in from across the expanse of disturbed water. Harry sat down heavily in his battered swivel chair. Tim sipped his hot tea and contemplated his plan of action for removing Jackdaw's engine. Zed and Dwain, in between eating biscuits and drinking cola, checked their phones for replies.

The loud thud when it came seemed to suck the oxygen from the office; windows shook violently in their frames and loose objects rattled and fell from shelves. Harry's mouth opened mechanically. He swung the chair to jump up, tripped then fell against the desk. Dwain leant over and grabbed his arm to steady him. Tim and Zed ran outside. They watched in horror as across the marina a cloud of thick black smoke interlaced with streaks of orange flame rose high into the morning sky.

Tim shouted to Harry. 'Call the fire service.'
Holding onto the door for support he turned and went back into the office.

Delayed by shock, panicked voices and distressed screams now came from the site of the blaze. Tim, Zed and Dwain ran along the service jetty, across the small grass mound and through the gate which led to the residential mooring. There were eight boats moored alongside narrow finger pontoons. The furthest, was barely visible through the thick, black, toxic cloud. Fortunately, it was the middle of the day and most of the residents were out at work.

A sobbing woman with cuts to her face ran past them, followed by a man carrying a spent fire extinguisher. 'It went up so quickly, there was nothing we could do,' he shouted. Tim asked if it was his boat. He shook his head. Before Tim could ask if anyone was aboard, they had disappeared through the gate to safety. Tim called to Zed and Dwain to untie all the boats and push them out into the marina. From the safety of a nearby grass banking, an elderly couple from the neighbouring boat watched as their windows cracked and the intense heat blistered their paintwork. The woman nursed a small shaking dog and sobbed as their home succumbed to the nearby inferno.

Holding his cap over his mouth Tim ran along the pontoon. He managed to untie the bow line of the couples, boat but could not reach the stern as the wooden finger pontoon had now caught fire.

The elderly man was waving his arms and shouting, 'Gas bottles. Gas bottles.'

A second explosion was what Tim had feared. He assumed, as with most boats, the bottles were in a bow locker. Having untied the line, he attempted to pull the bow away from the burning jetty. It would mean sacrificing the stern end to the flames, but better that than the intense heat reaching the gas bottles. At first it wouldn't budge. As he tugged splatters of hot ash were falling on his hands and face. He was on the point of giving up when there was an almighty crack as the burning finger pontoon collapsed into the water.

Suddenly the bow line went slack, and he was able to pull it over and tie it onto a mooring ring.

In the distance they could hear the sound of the approaching fire appliances. Zed and Dwain, with eyes smarting and blackened sweat running down their cheeks, pushed the last of the moored boats out into the marina. From behind them, red faced and puffing Harry asked, 'Is anybody hurt?
I say is.........?
Zed interrupted and shook his head. 'We don't know yet.'
Harry went past them along the pontoon then realised with horror whose craft it was.

'It's Roy Coombe's boat, I say it's Roy's. I was talking to him earlier.' His voice tapered off in despair.

Tim, who could do no more to help, walked towards him shaking his head. 'If he was on board it's too late, there's nothing to be done.' Harry buried his face in his hands.

Two fire appliances sped through the marina gates and screeched to a halt outside the office, their blue lights reflecting off the water. The doors flew open, and the volunteer fire crews from Melbury quickly exited.

It took an hour for the burning boat to be brought under control, leaving behind a smouldering, charred hull. Pieces of burnt debris floated nearby and a large oily diesel spill polluted the water. Since the arrival of the fire brigade other emergency services had descended on the scene, amongst them ambulances and a red van with 'Fire Investigation Unit' written on the side.

The question on everybody's lips now was the whereabouts of the boat's owner, Roy Coombs. As the firefighters gained access to the inside of the vessel that question would be answered sooner rather than later. But as his car was still in the marina everybody expected the worst.

Back in the office Harry sat slumped in his leather chair, beads of sweat collecting on his ghostly pallor. Tim, Zed and Dwain looked on anxiously as a female paramedic attached monitoring pads to his exposed chest. She turned to Tim. 'He's having a heart attack. We need to get him to hospital quickly.' Through the misted oxygen mask, Harry beckoned to Tim who leant in close to him touching him on the shoulder. The question came in a low struggled whisper.

'Course mate. We'll look after the place. Don't worry about it.'

Another paramedic arrived pulling a gurney. They carefully manoeuvred Harry from the chair onto the stretcher. Suddenly feeling tired Tim leant against the desk, the smell of acrid fumes still lingering in his nostrils. Zed and Dwain followed Harry to the waiting ambulance. He gave them a limp wave as they lifted him in the back.

'You alright?' Dwain asked Zed.

'I think so, just can't help thinking about that poor bloke on the boat.'

Dwain nodded. 'It's bad man, but we don't yet know if he was on board.'

They stepped over a bird's nest of uncoiled, thick red hoses, some connected to the rear of the fire appliances, others to a loud throbbing pump sucking water from the marina.

Zed's phone pinged. He took it from his pocket and studied the screen. It was a text message from George. CALL 2 NITE BFF

Dwain asked, 'Did he say why they're not coming?'

'Said he'd call later.'

Tim came out of the office. He could see a huddle of yellow helmeted firefighters at the far end of the pontoon. A second police car had arrived, and the plain clothed occupants were walking to meet them. An eerie calm had settled across the marina in stark contrast to the dramatic events of the last two hours. Swans moved sedately on the sun-sparkled water whilst boats bobbed gently against their moorings. Overhead puffy white clouds drifted slowly across a blue sky.

Dwain and Zed had sat down on the grass at the side of the access road. They watched as a firefighter in a white helmet and one of the recently arrived police officers walked back from the charred boat, through the gate and towards where Tim was standing. A small black kitten came through a hedge opposite and lay down purring against Dwain's leg. He stroked his soft fur.

'Now, who do you belong to?' he asked.

Their sullen faces said it all. The police officer asked if Tim was the marina manager.

He explained that the owner had been taken to hospital with a suspected heart attack and he was left in charge. The fire officer spoke. 'I'm afraid it's bad news, we've found a body on board.'

Tim shook his head. 'That's very sad.'

The police officer asked, 'Could you confirm the name of the owner?'

Tim beckoned them inside the office. He went to a tall green filing cabinet and pulled open a drawer marked MOORINGS.

Surprised, the officer said, 'That's an old-fashioned system.'

Tim smiled. 'Bit of a technophobe, our Harry.' He flicked through the hanging files then pulled out one marked 'MOORING SIXTY EIGHT.' Before opening it, he said, 'I think you'll find the boat belonged to a Roy Coombs. The officer held out his hand and Tim passed him the file. Glancing through it he read aloud slowly. 'Roy Coombs. Narrowboat Noggin. Paid one year in advance 14th February.' As there were other personal details in the file pertaining to the victim he asked if he could take it.

'Sure, it won't be needed anymore,' replied Tim, closing the filing cabinet drawer.

The kitten followed Zed and Dwain back to the office. 'Who's this then?' asked Tim bending down to stroke it. His hand was almost the size of the small creature. Zed smiled. 'I think he's adopted us.'

'What's the latest?' asked Dwain.

With a weary sigh Tim replied, 'It's not good. They've found a body and it looks like it's Roy Coombs.'

# CHAPTER FOURTEEN

## Top Secret

A few days later Rocket Ron left the offices of the Melbury Echo clutching the buff coloured folder which the editor, Sharon Giddings, had given him earlier. It had been a long morning and he was feeling hungry. On the opposite side of the market square was the popular Milan Café run by Guiseppe Amato, his wife and daughter. Ron was a regular visitor. He nodded to some people he knew sitting at the outside tables and went in. On market day the place would be heaving, but now just a few of the regulars pawed through their newspapers or stared obsessively at their mobile phones. He sat at a table by the window and flicked through the comprehensive menu. It had to be an all day breakfast and a mug of tea.

With excited anticipation he opened the folder, careful not to let anyone near him see the contents. Would this lead him closer to the disappearance of Daisy Kearns all those years ago? Inside were several sheets of paper. The typewritten text, like his eyes, was dulled by age. Taking his glasses from his pocket, his heart missed a beat as he read the header on each sheet.

**MINISTRY OF WAR – TOP SECRET DOCUMENTS
July 1944.**

He flicked through to the last two sheets, which unlike the others were not text but a grainy black and white picture, stapled to an equally faded map. Hearing footsteps behind him he quickly closed the folder and turned around. An attractive young woman with long black hair and striking blue eyes brought his meal to the table, along with a mug of tea bearing the national flag of Italy.

He smiled at her. 'Grazie Sofia.'

She giggled. 'Prego, signore Ron. Prego.'

Full up with a meal which would last him all day he said goodbye to Guiseppe and Sofia and left the comfortable ambiance of the small café. His aching legs would not sustain the walk back along the towpath, so he went to the taxi rank outside the town hall. He knew most of the drivers. Standing by the front car, was a small Polish man. 'Hey, good to see you,' he called as Ron approached the parked silver Toyota. Ron smiled wearily. 'And you Marek.'

The taxi didn't take long to reach its destination. Ron fought the urge to fall asleep. Soon they had turned off the road and were bumping along the track towards the abandoned Muckle Farm. Looking around the deserted yard and farmhouse Marek asked, 'I often wonder, is this where you live Ron?'

He laughed. 'No, I have a narrowboat moored on the canal.'

Marek seemed reassured and tooted the horn as he headed back to Melbury. Ron went through the gate held to the post by one broken hinge and climbed down the grass banking onto the towpath, where his boat was moored astern of Rose's.

She was outside cleaning the windows, her white hair blowing in the stiff breeze. Ron's two ferrets, Frankie and Freddie, were scampering about round her feet. He whistled and they both ran towards him. Bending down he scooped up one in each hand.

Rose asked, 'Worthwhile visit, was it?'

He nodded. 'Very interesting.'

'I'll put the kettle on then you can tell me all about it,' she said, going into the boat.

Ron followed her clutching the folder tightly. As usual the pungent smell of boiling herbs permeated the air. Ron hated drinking the bitter liquid, but if it helped his arthritic knees then so be it. They both sat at the table which was covered by a thick maroon cloth.

Underneath, was the wooden trunk where Rose kept all her abandoned bears. Frankie and Freddie had curled up on the rug by the fireplace. Ron opened the folder and spread the contents out across the table cloth. Rose was immediately startled by the words **TOP SECRET** stamped across each sheet.

'Where did Sharon Giddings get these from?' she asked anxiously.

Ron chuckled. 'Best not to ask too many questions.' He pointed to the grainy black and white map. 'What do you make of that?'

Putting on her glasses she picked it up and moved it closer to her eyes. 'It's quite faded.'

Ron laughed. 'Well, it is over seventy years old.'

She studied it for a few minutes, occasionally rotating it one way then another. Enthusiastically he pointed to a small area on the map circled in red ink and marked Ivy House.

'Do you recognise anything there?'

She shook her head. 'Sorry Ron, I don't, and I've never heard of an Ivy House around here.'

Placing the map and picture next to each other on the table, she scanned her eyes keenly between the two then tapped her finger on the photo image. 'You see there, by the bend in that road. It looks like a wide gap between the hedgerows. You can just make out the tall gates.'

Ron came round the table and looked over her shoulder. 'Could it be the entrance to a large house?'

Rose shrugged. 'The only big old house I know of round here is the Manor House where the Barrington Gores live'. She took off her glasses and rubbed her eyes. 'You need to talk to either Tim or Peggy, they were born and brought up here. If anyone can recognise where it is, they will.'

Ron agreed. 'Good idea. In the meantime, I'll study the other documents.'

As he stood to go, Rose took a brochure from a drawer in the table and slid it across to him.

'What's this?' he asked, picking up the glossy publication.

She apprehensively waited to see his reaction as he digested the front cover.

'The Orchard Sheltered Housing Complex,' he said, in a surprised tone.

She nodded. 'What do you think?'

He sat back down at the table. 'With regards to what?' he asked, somewhat confused.

'To me moving in there.'

He was almost speechless, stuttering, 'What, Why? You can't give up the.......'

She held up her hand. 'Ron, listen to me. Neither of us is getting any younger and I am finding living on the boat harder with each year that passes.'

He interrupted. 'Yes, but......'

Again, she stopped him. 'Of course, I shall miss the boat, but it's better to make the move while I'm still mobile.'

He said nothing. Then sighed deeply. 'I do understand,' he mumbled.

She leant across the table and took his hand in her pale stick like fingers. 'Ron you are and will always be my closest friend, and I love you very much.' He looked up into her seasoned wrinkled face then smiled. 'And I you.'

For a few moments neither spoke. Then Rose said, 'Why don't I make another cuppa?' His face brightened and he laughed. 'After that shock I'll need a strong one.'

A darkness of mood fell upon him as he walked back to his boat. Frankie and Freddie chased a squirrel across the grass banking. In his heart he knew Rose was right. She had become frailer ever since Zed's Uncle Darren and his accomplice had forced their way into her boat, attempting to steal the Golden Windlass which old Mr Coote had gifted her.

Overhead he watched the flying grey clouds as the late afternoon sky ebbed gradually towards dusk. He shuddered. The thought of living alone again on the towpath filled him full of horror. Inside the boat he fed Frankie and Freddie before shutting them in their cage for the night. Pulling his coat tightly around him he sank wearily into his armchair, the Daisy Kearns folder resting on his knee. Soon he fell into a deep sleep with only his fitful dreams to keep him company. Here he remained until the chill of the morning woke him.

Amongst the awfulness of the day, Zed allowed himself a laugh when Dwain jumped from one boat to another, slipped and nearly fell into the water. It had been one thing to push all the narrowboats out into the marina, quite another to retrieve them afterwards. Fortunately, Harry had a Dory with an outboard motor, but even with Tim at the helm it was a challenge for them to manoeuvre the narrowboats in the stiff breeze which always seemed to blow across the open space.

The fire service had covered the hull of the burnt out boat with a large red plastic sheet. Blue and white police tape sealed off the immediate area. All the emergency vehicles had now left the scene, the last being the Fire Investigation Unit whose crew had spent ages trying to determine the cause of the fire. Other marina residents had now returned home from work. Shocked at the news they stood in little huddles trying to make sense of it all.

Tim nudged the last recovered narrowboat into place. Zed and Dwain jumped off the bow and made it fast against the pontoon. With an urgent burst of power on the twist grip, Tim turned the Dory sharply and headed back across the marina. Waves of wash sloshed against the moored boats rocking them from side to side. After securing the Dory against the service jetty he cut the twenty horse power engine then sat for a few moments staring out across the now peaceful vista.

Inside Harry's office papers were strewn across the floor. Two part finished mugs of cold tea stood on the cluttered desk, ignored as the explosion had rocked the office. Harry's leather chair had been knocked sideways as the paramedics had lifted him onto the gurney. Tim switched on the light. Overhead the starter crackled as the fluorescent bulb illuminated, flooding the room with a bright cold glare. He went into the small adjoining kitchen. Picking up the kettle to fill it he noticed a tremor in his hands. It was only then that the full horror and revulsion of the day's tragic incident caught up with him. He steadied himself against the sink, breathing deeply to control his raw emotions.

Zed and Dwain sat on the wooden bench outside the office, their young bodies racked with fatigue. Zed rubbed his sore, gritty eyes, his face and hands, like Dwain's, scorched with falling ash and stained by thick oily smoke. Dwain went inside and took two cans of cola from the cooler.

'You two alright?' asked Tim, emerging from the kitchen.

Dwain nodded. 'We're knackered.'

Tim laughed. 'I know how you feel.'

He followed Dwain outside and sat alongside them both on the bench.

Zed asked. 'Have you heard how Harry is?'

Tim shook his head. 'Not yet. Peggy said she would call as soon as she heard any news.'

Dwain felt something rub against his leg. He bent down, scooped up the small black kitten and put it on his lap. 'Hello. You here again?'

'I expect it belongs to one of the boaters,' said Zed stroking it.

Dwain grinned. 'I think we should kidnap it, take it back to the boat.' He picked the kitten up and stared into its face. 'Would you like to come home with us, one miaow for yes, two for no.'

Zed shook his head.

# CHAPTER FIFTEEN

## The Aftermath

Before it rang, Tim's mobile phone vibrated in the pocket of his oily overalls. Clumsily he fumbled to find it before the answerphone clicked in. He hated listening to those messages, complaining that people always spoke too fast. The boys laughed as he pulled out the old Nokia and flipped it open to talk. Peggy's voice was subdued. Fearing the worst of news Tim asked, 'What's happened?' Peggy said she had spoken to the hospital. Harry was stable but they needed to operate on his heart. Shocked by the suddenness of the reply, Tim asked, 'What? When?'

'Tomorrow. It can't wait, he has coronary artery disease.'

Tim sighed. 'The old devil didn't see that one coming.'

'Maybe he did.'

She asked how the boys were doing. He chuckled. 'I'm sure they've had better days.'

He said goodbye to her, flicked the phone shut and dropped it into his top pocket.

'I can't believe it, Harry's got to have an urgent heart op.'

'Man, that sounds pretty heavy,' Dwain replied.

Tim nodded. 'You could say that lad.'

Zed added, 'Blimey, poor old Harry.'

The little black kitten jumped off Dwain's lap and ran towards the grass banking.

Zed laughed. 'He's going home for his tea.'

Tim yawned. 'So are we. Come on, time and tide......'

He switched off the office light, pulled down the blinds and locked the door. Zed and Dwain had already jumped into the passenger seat of the Land Rover. Before climbing in beside them Tim checked Harry's new Volvo was secure. As they turned out of the marina onto the narrow lane, Zed asked. 'How long will Harry be away?' Tim crunched into third gear.

'Who knows, it could be at least four months.' Nobody said much more for the remainder of the journey home, they were too tired to talk.

Peggy and Zed's gran, Betty, were waiting for them as the Land Rover shuddered to a halt outside the cottage. 'Good grief,' exclaimed Peggy, startled by their blackened appearance.

Betty said, 'You both look like you've been working down a coal mine.'

Zed smiled at her. 'We feel like it too Gran.'

Tim didn't follow the boys inside the cottage. Instead, he sat on the bench outside the window and breathed in the clean fresh air. Peggy joined him. 'You ok love?'

He nodded slowly. 'Yeah, but it was pretty awful; and that poor man.'

Resting her hand on his, she noticed the pitted burn marks from the hot, falling ash.

'How about a nice strong brew.'

Smiling he replied, 'Just the job Peg.' Then mimicking Harry, said, 'I say, just the job.'

They both laughed.     Betty had organised the boys. Their soiled clothes had been discarded to the laundry basket and they had disappeared into a steamy bathroom to get showered. Outside Peggy passed Tim his mug of tea. He took a large sip. 'Wow, that's some strong brew.'

She laughed. 'I thought an added wee dram would perk you up.'

Betty giggled as the boys came into the sitting room clad only in bath towels. 'You look like a pair of lobsters.' Although in fact Zed's freckled Celtic skin looked a lot redder than Dwain's. They both sat on the sofa then Zed said, 'We haven't got any spare clothes here Gran.'

'Yes, you have, I brought some back from the flat today; all washed and pressed.'

She went into the kitchen and returned with a large bag.

Dwain laughed. 'Thanks for that. I didn't fancy running naked along the towpath to the boat.'

'Ah, that's better,' said Peggy, coming into the room from outside. 'You two look almost human now.' The boys took the bag of clothes into Zed's old bedroom to get dressed. Peggy shouted after them, 'I'll make you a sandwich, keep you both going until dinner.'

Tim finished his tea and sat listening to the calming sound of the water seeping through the lock gates. The breeze which had hampered them at the marina earlier had dropped and the air was still. In Tiddledurn the clock on St Mark's church tower struck seven. He looked across at Barney's grave underneath the apple tree. This was when he missed his old collie the most, just the two of them sitting quietly in the still of the evening. He felt a lump forming in his throat and swallowed hard to remove it.

He contemplated the impact of Harry's heart attack, and the length of time he would be out of action. Apart from his niece there was no other family ever spoken of. He sighed. There was nothing to be done until Harry could receive visitors and he could talk to him.

Groaning, he lifted himself up from the bench. His back was not getting any better which did not bode well for the future. He pulled open the front door, and entered the warm sitting room. The welcome aroma of something delicious cooking wafted from the kitchen.

Zed lay sprawled on the sofa wearing a bottle green tracksuit, his head moving rhythmically to the music blasting from his earphones. Dwain in a sweatshirt and jogging bottoms was hunched over the table playing candy crush on his phone. Tim smiled at this picture of domestic bliss. They were good kids and he was proud of how they had responded to the tragedy at the marina. He just never seemed to get round to telling them.

'I'm going for a shower,' he called to Peggy. There was a muffled reply from behind the closed kitchen door. 'Don't be long, dinner's nearly ready.'

The boys had been starving. Twice Betty scolded them for gobbling their food.
Tim mopped up the last of the gravy with a thick piece of tiger bread. 'Ah, that was good. Homemade shepherd's pie, you can't beat it.' Zed teased Dwain, reminding him that once he didn't know what shepherd's pie was.

He shrugged. 'Yeah, well you never knew what jerk chicken was either.'
Betty looked confused. 'Nor do I love. What is it?'

'It's a Jamaican thing, Gran. Spicy meat served with rice.' He now affectionately called Betty Gran. She was pleased as she regarded him as a second grandson.

Peggy said, 'Sounds nice, we'll have to try it one evening.'

Tim wasn't so convinced about this foreign fare idea. Noting his distain, she added, 'You're an old stick in the mud fuddy duddy.'
He stood up from the table and patted his full tummy. 'And happy to be so.'
Dwain asked, 'What's a fuddy duddy?'
Peggy laughed. 'Someone who's old fashioned and fussy, love.'
Betty caught Zed's eye, 'Don't you dare say a word.'

The incoming calls on their phones came within seconds of each other. The boys both went outside the cottage and stood some distance apart from each other on the lawn. Tim settled into his armchair by the unlit fireplace. 'I bet that's those Barrington Gore kids.'

Both George and Phoebe gave the same story as to why they couldn't go on the boat trip with them. Their parents had arranged for them to spend a few days with their maternal grandmother in Sidmouth, where she had a house on the seafront. Whilst Zed was prepared to accept this plausible excuse, Dwain though was more sceptical of the reason. He thought Lady Barrington Gore had probably prevented it, as Phoebe would be the only girl on board.
He chuckled to himself, 'Another fuddy duddy.'
Though he didn't suggest this to Phoebe. She told him that she and George had heard about the boat explosion at the marina.

Dwain asked how they knew. 'My mother, she heard it on the local radio.' He told her that he and Zed were there when it had happened. She gushed with concern. 'Oh my god, you poor thing. Are you alright?' He loved to hear her 'posh' clipped tone of voice. Respectfully he said, 'Yeah, we are, but that poor man died and Harry's had a heart attack.'

She asked who Harry was. Dwain explained that he owned the marina and is an old friend of Tim and Peggy. There was silence for a moment then she said softly. 'I really wish I was there with you. I could give you a little cuddle.' He smiled at the thought of it. 'That would be cool Pheebs.'

George was not happy. He had been looking forward to spending time with Zed on the narrowboat trip. 'I can think of nothing more boring than staying with my grandmother in Sidmouth. I mean, it's full of old crusties.' Zed laughed at that description of the inhabitants of the coastal town. Then he said,' I shall miss you.'

George chuckled. 'Likewise, dude.'

Peggy waited until Zed and Dwain came back indoors before she walked Betty back across the village green to her flat above Strout's butcher's shop. The boys stayed a little longer talking to Tim who kept nodding off in the armchair. He hadn't asked about the phone calls, and they never said. Pitch darkness had swallowed the canal by the time they left the cottage to walk back to Turtle. Even with Tim's powerful torch they didn't dawdle along the towpath, unnerved by the clattering branches and nocturnal sounds as unseen creatures rustled in the undergrowth.

As they approached Turtle, Tim's two community boats Odin and Thor were just visible through the gloom. Zed shone the torch onto their trad sterns. Moored in front of Turtle, opposite the old stables, the seventy foot canvas topped boats reminded Zed of two great tethered beasts. This saddened him as he remembered the fun times on board and the many characters he had met on various journeys.

Dwain said. 'It seems like ages since they've been out with a group.'

Zed refocused the torch beam onto the bow of Turtle. 'It's a shame. Tim and Peggy seem to be too busy with other things now.'

Dwain unzipped the cratch cover, stepped over the gunwales and went inside. 'Do you think we're still going to Boswell's Yard with the boats?'

Following him, Zed shrugged. 'Dunno dude. Tim hasn't said anything and we're back to school on Monday.'

Dwain groaned. 'Don't remind me.' They had both lived happily aboard Peggy's narrowboat now for some time, and whilst it afforded them freedom and independence, having only one sleeping quarter was proving restrictive. Although they had adopted one another as honorary siblings, sharing a double bed, albeit in sleeping bags was proving not ideal now for two teenage boys.

They stumbled through the darkened saloon and into the stern cabin. Both boys were mentally and physically exhausted. Throwing off their clothes they climbed wearily into their sleeping bags. Dwain turned off the sidelight and in minutes sleep had overtaken them.

# CHAPTER SIXTEEN

## The Old Lifestyle

Smokey Joe studied the name printed at the bottom of the letter which he had recently received from Melbury Town Council. He sniffed contemptuously. 'What sort of a name is that? Quinton Drake!' He and Ben, the carpenter, were sitting on the wooden bench in the garden of old Mr Coote's cottage, which Smokey had now inherited. Ben had driven over earlier that morning from the Manor House where he was replacing the wooden staircase leading down to the cellar. Used by the family for many years as storage, Lady Barrington Gore had decided to clear out the generations of clutter occupying the below stairs cavern.

The council official arrived promptly at twelve, striding purposefully towards the two waiting men. Tucked under his arm was the obligatory clip board, the other hand holding a small hiking type rucksack. 'I'm looking for the owner of the property, a Mr…..' he paused and consulted the document on his clipboard, 'Ah yes, Joseph Aldridge.'

'That's me,' answered Smokey, not attempting to disguise his dislike of 'jobsworth' and petty officials. Ben smiled as he noticed the man's predictable reaction to Smokey's unorthodox appearance. As usual he was wearing his wide brimmed hat with pheasant feather, long ex-army greatcoat tied around the waist by a length of string and black boots. His long unkempt beard clung to his chin like a resting furry animal.

Unzipping his green fleece adorned with the council logo the official flashed a plastic badge attached to a red lanyard. 'Quinton Drake,' he proclaimed loudly. 'I'm here to carry out your electrical inspection.'

As with many other areas of the old pre-war property the wiring was not fit for purpose. Ben had recruited a local electrician friend of his to undertake the work. He had been shocked by the poor condition suggesting it could have caught fire at any moment. This time-consuming piece of work had further delayed the moving in date. Not that Smokey was too troubled by this; it afforded him more time to validate this life changing decision.

Smokey stood up from the bench. 'This way then.'

Quinton Drake followed the two men across the lawn and up the steps onto the recently renovated veranda.

'Help yourself,' said Smokey, pointing to the double glass doors. Quinton Drake took a red and white spotted handkerchief from his pocket and blew his beak-like nose. Then bending down he unzipped the rucksack and pulled out a white forensic-style protective suit.

Smokey couldn't resist a sarcastic quip. 'The body is in the bathroom, Gil Grissom.'

The council official continued dressing without reacting to this comedic provocation. Smokey raised his eyes in despair.

Ben whispered, 'I doubt he's ever seen CSI Crime Scene.'

Returning to the clipboard Quinton Drake flicked over the first page of an attached A4 document.

Tapping it with his pen, he said, 'Providing all these boxes have a tick then I can raise a certificate of compliance.' He paused for effect. 'However, if there are any crosses….' He gave a wry smile, 'Well, we'll have to see.'

After he had disappeared through the doors Ben asked, 'Was he looking for a bribe?'

Smokey laughed. 'He's out of luck if he was.' Over an hour had passed before Quinton Drake emerged, his forensic clothing brushed with dirt and dust.

Again, Smokey couldn't resist. 'Find any rats?'

Quinton Drake sighed. 'No sir, but there is evidence of mice infestation. You would do well to call in pest control.'

Smokey chuckled. 'Don't worry about it. They'll keep me company in the evening.'

'So, what's the verdict?' asked Ben. His words hung unanswered in the air whilst Quinton removed his outer garment. Then as if relishing the suspense, he picked up the clipboard and flicked slowly through the A4 document until he reached the last page.

'I have to say that your man did a good job and everything complies with the current regulations.'

Ben nodded. 'Good, thanks for that mate.' There was a flicker of irritation at this over familiarity. Turning to Smokey, Quinton tapped the bottom of the page with his biro. 'I require a signature here please.'

Smokey signed. Quinton Blake tucked the clipboard under his arm then picked up his rucksack. 'Well gentlemen that concludes our business. The certificate will be sent to you within ten days.' He turned to go. 'I bid you both farewell.'

The two men watched from the veranda as he crossed the garden. Smokey shook his head. 'I bid you both farewell ! Why can't he just say goodbye like any normal person?'

Ben laughed. 'Because they're all programmed like robots.'

The double doors led directly from the veranda into the spacious lounge with dark oak rafted ceiling. From a window a shaft of bright light arced across the hollow interior, particles of dust dancing within the golden beam. Much of the furniture, which like its previous owner had grown old and tired, had been removed. A faded, elaborately patterned Persian rug lay in front of the red brick fireplace. Above its arch a blackened soot stain snaked along the stack, testament to many years of winter log burning.

Smokey fondly remembered as a boy laying on the rug in his pyjamas whilst his aunt toasted crumpets on the crackling fire. His uncle, never one for television, sat in his deep armchair with his favourite Briar pipe clasped between his teeth. He recalled the wonderful aromatic smell of his Clan tobacco as the smoke lingered like a cloud above the room.

But that was yesteryear, a time of childhood innocence. Since then, much turbulent water had flowed under many bridges; each current taking a little piece of him with it. Now as he stood with his memories a sad coldness seemed to have settled over the once comforting and welcoming abode. A corpse, whose soul had long departed.

Ben was on his hands and knees inspecting a section of broken skirting board when Smokey suddenly asked. 'When do you think a house becomes a home and not just a pile of bricks and mortar, or worse a quick investment?'

Ben stood up and brushed the dust from his knees. 'Wow mate, that's a bit deep for a Monday morning.' He thought for a moment. 'I suppose it's the people who live there, the noise and laughter; all that goes with family life.' He chuckled, 'particularly with kids running about the place.'

Smokey nodded. 'Home is where the heart is.'

'Yeah, you could say that mate.'

Smokey's sudden abruptness surprised Ben. 'Come on let's go.' Stepping out onto the veranda Smokey closed and locked the doors. He stood for a moment looking out across the garden which his aunt had so lovingly tended. On the far side the tangled woods disguised the hide where he and his uncle had spent many long hours observing the bird and wildlife.

Sensing a change in Smokey's mood Ben asked, 'You alright mate?'

At first, he didn't answer the carpenter's question. 'Just thoughts Ben, just thoughts.'

Walking back along the track towards the gate Ben said. 'I have some news.'

Smokey stopped. 'What's that then? Is it good or bad?'

Smiling broadly Ben said, 'Remi's pregnant.'

Smokey's eyes opened wide with delight. 'Oh Ben, that's wonderful.' He placed his hand on Ben's shoulder. 'You'll make a great dad.' He paused. 'What's the bad news then?'

'We're going to have to sell the boat.'

Smokey was shocked. 'Sell it! What for?'

Ben laughed. 'You've obviously never had to bring a baby up on a boat. Remi would be a bag of nerves.'

Smokey chuckled. 'That's true. But where will you live?'

'We'd have to rent somewhere in Melbury.' He hesitated. 'Look mate I'm not keen on the idea, we both love the boat, but it just wouldn't be practical.'

After going through the gate which led onto the towpath Smokey attached a padlock to the chain and snapped it shut. Ben had parked his van a short distance away in the small car park alongside the lock. Smokey decided to walk with him then call in to see Tim and Peggy afterwards.

It had been a week since the fatal explosion at Harry Martin's marina. News of the incident had spread quickly along the canal, as had the part Tim, Zed and Dwain played in the unfolding tragedy. Reaching the car park Smokey shook his head in disbelief as he saw a 'fly tipped' mattress leaning against some trees. 'What is it with these people?'

'They're scumbags,' replied Ben, opening the door of the van. Then lowering himself into the driver's seat, he turned to Smokey. 'You still seem unsure about moving into your uncle's cottage mate.' Smokey smiled but said nothing. Ben waved as he drove away. Smokey called after him. 'Look after that little lady of yours.'

He crossed over the lock gates leading to Tim's canal side cottage. Sammy and Sheena, the two swans were sleeping on the grass bank, their long necks tucked deep inside their plumage. Closing his eyes, he breathed in deeply then looking skywards said, 'Well Driftwood me old mate, it's back to the same old lifestyle. But then you knew that all along, didn't you?'

Tim emerged from the side of the cottage carrying a twenty litre Jerry can. 'Get off my lawn, you old vagrant.'

Smokey laughed. 'I don't mind the vagrant, but not so much of the old.'

'Have you come from the cottage?' Tim asked.

'Yeah, me and Ben had to meet some council jobsworth about the electrics.'

Tim chuckled, 'There's plenty of them about.' He left the Jerry can on the step and they both went inside. Smokey removed his coat and hat. 'It's quiet in here.'

'Great isn't it? The boys are back at school and Peg and Betty have gone trawling through charity shops in Melbury. You fancy a brew?'

'Thought you'd never ask.'

Smokey relaxed into the comfortable sofa and closed his eyes. Tim returned with two mugs of strong tea. Smokey blinked awake.

'You ok mate?' Tim asked.

He emitted a deep sigh. 'I'm alright, just a lot on my mind. Anyway, enough about me. How are you? I heard about the fire in the marina, must have been awful.'

Tim sat in his armchair then took a mouthful of tea. 'In all my time on the waterways I've never seen anything like it. Frightening how quickly the boat went up.'

'How's Harry?'

'He's had the operation to clear the blockage in his heart and is stable, although we still can't visit him,' he replied.

Smokey shook his head. 'You just never know what's around the corner.'

Tim agreed then quickly changed the subject. 'So, what's happening with the house then?'

Smokey hesitated before answering. His gaze fixed somewhere on the low ceiling.

'You know what, Tim? Ever since I was summoned to the solicitors in Melbury, I've had this lead weight around my neck.' He looked crestfallen. 'Terrible isn't it? Most people would be over the moon, grateful at such an inheritance. But it's just not for me.' He half smiled. 'What the devil would I do rattling around that place on my own?'

Tim was trying to make sense of his old friend's dilemma. 'Is it because of Driftwood's passing, or something else?'

Smokey nodded sadly. 'Partly that. He was looking forward to living out his days there. But he's gone. Also......' He paused. 'I'm on my own here Tim, just me and my demons and nothing's going to change that.' He laughed. 'We've learned to live together as we are.'

Feeling his melancholy Tim said. 'It's nearly lunchtime. We've got some freshly made bread. How about a nice ham sandwich and a fresh brew?'

'That'll be good mate, ta.' Smokey smiled, 'Plenty of mustard please.'

As Tim made for the kitchen, he once again closed his eyes and relaxed into the cushioned folds.

After lunch the two men sat outside the cottage overlooking the double lock. Meditative trickles of water fell gently into the chamber from the canal above. The warm late May sun massaged their leathery skins. A Red Admiral butterfly fluttered close to them, then in a flash of colour it was gone.

Tim and Smokey had known each other for many years and these two complex souls were happy in each other's company.

'What will you do with the house if you don't live there?' Tim asked.

Before answering, Smokey slowly stroked the straggly ends of his long greying beard. 'I think I have a plan.'

'Which is?'

I'm going to let it out to Ben and Remi at a peppercorn rent.'

Tim was surprised by the answer. 'Why them?'

'Remi is pregnant and they're going to have to sell the boat.'

Tim nodded. 'That makes a lot of sense with a new baby.'

Smokey continued. 'Ben's plan is to rent some rabbit hutch in Melbury which will no doubt cost them a fortune each month.'

Tim thought about the idea for a moment. 'Are you really sure this is what you want to do?'

Smokey's face brightened. 'I am Tim. Don't you see they will bring love and life back to the old place. Something I could never do.'

Tim placed his hand firmly on Smokey's arm and smiled. 'You're a soft-hearted devil beneath that earthy layer my friend.'

# CHAPTER SEVENTEEN

## The Cellar

Zed and Dwain sat either side of George on the back seat of Lady Barrington Gore's Range Rover. Phoebe sat next to her mother in the front passenger seat. It was certainly more comfortable than Tim's old Series One Land Rover. In the back Milo and Morgan, the two black Labradors, slobbered happily over a large bone.

The first few days of school after the half term break had been a slog. After finishing on the Thursday afternoon Phoebe and George had invited Zed and Dwain back to the Manor House. They were keen to show off their new 'cellar den' which was to be their own teenage space. The boys had decided to say nothing to their new friends about their forebear's controversial dark past. As Dwain had said, 'They probably don't know anything about it anyway. Why should they? It was a long time ago.'

Above the classical music playing on the car radio, Lady Barrington Gore asked, 'I understand from the children that you both live on a narrowboat. That must be terribly exciting?'

Dwain met her enquiring gaze in the interior mirror. He could see where Phoebe got her striking blue eyes from. 'We stay there at night. We don't live on it all the time,' he said.

'Oh, I see. And Tim and Peggy, are they your parents?'

Dwain was just about to explain when Phoebe interrupted sharply. 'It's complicated Mummy.' Recognising her daughter's subtle request to be quiet she said nothing more on the subject.

A few miles from Tiddledurn where she had earlier met them off the school bus, the Range Rover turned off the road, crunched along the tree-lined gravel driveway before stopping in front of the main entrance. Dwain and Zed had often wondered what the Manor House looked like, but they were still impressed at the size of the three-storey stately pile. When Lady Barrington Gore opened the back hatch Milo and Morgan leapt barking from the vehicle and ran quickly into nearby undergrowth.

'Come on,' said Phoebe, taking Dwain's hand and leading him up the steps. This display of affection did not escape Lady Barrington Gore. George and Zed were less demonstrative as they went through the solid oak door into the cavernous circular hallway.

Dwain whispered to Zed. 'You could fit my old London flat in here.'

Before removing her battered Barbour jacket Lady Barrington Gore took a small metal whistle from the pocket. After three shrill blasts Milo and Morgan thundered across the hallway following her to a door on the opposite side. Phoebe chuckled. 'Dinner time.'

George nudged Zed. 'Come on, this way.' Dwain and Phoebe followed them along a narrow passageway between the sweeping staircase with highly polished bannisters and a wall lined with heavy framed pictures. Dwain stopped to look at one, a hay cart sitting in the middle of a pond. Phoebe said, 'It's a Constable,' then laughed, 'though they're not originals, unfortunately.'

At the end of the passage were two doors. George stopped at the one on the left. Pushing it open he groped inside for the light switch and turned it on.

As the rich aroma of wood brushed with linseed rose upwards,
he said, 'We've just had a new staircase fitted.' Then he chuckled 'my Dad's foot went through the other one.'

As they descended the now stable steps George asked, 'So, what do you think?'
Dwain and Zed exchanged a bemused look at the small musty smelling cluttered space.
Phoebe laughed. 'I know what you are thinking, but you have to look beyond the rubbish, that will be gone soon. Mummy has some men with a van coming.'

'And Dad's having heating and power points put in,' added George eagerly.

Zed asked, 'With all the rooms in the house couldn't you use one of those?'
Phoebe shook her head, the ends of her long brown hair swishing across her shoulders.

'No silly. Some of the rooms are in a worse state than this.'
George added. 'That's why we don't use the top floor of the house anymore.'
Phoebe continued, 'Anyway, down here nobody can hear our music, which Daddy's always complaining about.' She paused, fixing her blue eyes onto Dwain. 'There's just one problem, we have to decorate it ourselves. We were wondering if you would help us?'

Dwain looked at Zed and they both nodded.

'Course we will,' replied Dwain.
She bent forward and kissed him on the cheek. 'Thanks D, it'll be cool.'

Lady Barrington Gore appeared at the top of the stairs. Her Barbour jacket had been swapped for a blue padded body warmer.

The boys had noticed that even at this time of year there was a chill to the house. 'Time for tea everyone. Come along.'

In the centre of the spacious kitchen stood a long wooden table with a bleached surface and stout legs, the flagstone floor bearing the marks from generations of footfall. Along one wall was a French dresser laden with decorative plates and bowls. A cream cast iron AGA cooker hugged the space next to a huge fireplace, now disused. Every conceivable size of copper pot and pan hung from a suspended rack like recently shot pheasants waiting to be plucked. The high window above the farmhouse sink looked out across an expansive lawn bordered by summer perennials. At the furthest point a wooden gate led to a wild orchard.

The tea was sumptuous. Homemade fruit or cheese scones, ham sandwiches, bite size scotch eggs and squares of rich fruit cake. Lubrication was by way of lemonade and fresh orange juice. Lady Barrington Gore poured her Earl Grey tea from a warmed China teapot. She was keen to know more about the boy's background but decided it would keep for later. Having consumed their dinner, the two dogs, Milo and Morgan, slept soundly in their beds.

After the youngsters had eaten their fill, Lady Barrington Gore suggested running them home before it got dark. Phoebe and George wanted to go along for the ride but were firmly reminded they had homework to do, so they said goodbye on the doorstep. Zed was pleased that he was sitting in the back seat of the Range Rover when Lady Barrington Gore again asked, 'So, tell me about yourselves,' which sounded more like an order than a request. At first neither boy said a word.

Then Dwain, suspecting the reason for this fishing exercise, said, with a hint of irritation at her persistence. 'How long you got?'

Slightly taken aback by his tone, she said, 'Oh, dear it does sound.........'

Dwain interrupted her, 'Complicated, as Phoebe explained before.'

Listening to Dwain's mischievous evasion, Zed became concerned that she might take offence causing problems for George and Phoebe, so he explained to her the circumstances which had originally brought them to Tiddledurn; their relationship with Tim and Peggy, and the London gang which had pursued his gran. She was silent as he spoke, clearly shocked at the description of this parallel world of which she knew nothing and was never likely to experience. Arriving at the cottage the boys thanked her and jumped out. Before closing the door Dwain said cheekily. 'Funny life i'n it?'

She smiled and drove away.

Peggy called from the kitchen. 'I doubt you two want any dinner after partaking in high tea at the Barrington Gores.'

They were inclined to say no but were seduced by the smell of the lamb chops sizzling under the grill.

'Well, well,' said Betty laying the table. 'You two really have come up in the world.'

It was nearly seven o'clock in the evening and having been dropped back to the cottage Zed and Dwain, still in their school uniforms, were sitting on the sofa recounting their visit to Tim. He had not long returned from Harry Martin's marina where he had begun to remove Jackdaw's engine, a job he had intended to start on the day of the explosion.

Sitting opposite his gran at the dinner table Zed thought how much healthier and even younger she looked since moving here from London. She often entertained them with stories of the more colourful customers at Jean's canal shop where she now worked part time.

'Are you going to continue the story about the Barrington Gores later?' Zed asked Tim.
He stretched and yawned. 'Normal rules apply lad, normal rules apply.' Zed groaned and went to make him a strong brew. Dwain cleared away the dirty plates and followed him to the kitchen. Tim moved from the table to his armchair and poured himself a wee dram. Peggy said, 'The boys seem to have struck up a good friendship with George and Phoebe.'
With a sigh of resignation Tim nodded. 'Time and tide, and all that….'

After handing Tim his mug of tea the boys sat on the rug by the fireplace. Tim poured the last drop of the whisky from the glass into his tea. 'So where were we?'

'You were about to tell us if Edgar's brother Wilf ever came back to England,' said Zed.

'Ah yes, that's right; the illusive Wilf. Now don't forget that he fled to Munich in early 1939. Later that year on September 1st Hitler invaded Poland, then Britain and France declared war on Germany. So even though he was a British citizen it would have been very difficult for him to return to this country. Therefore, most people assumed he wouldn't. Then in 1942 something very strange happened. Tuesday was parade night at Tiddledurn village hall for the Local Defence Force, later called the Home Guard, or Dad's Army, as people got to know it.' Tim chuckled.

'Anyway, Albert Cook closed his garage early so he could be there for six o'clock.'

'He was the one who had threatened to kill Wilf for getting his daughter Alice pregnant?' asked Zed.

Tim nodded. 'That's right lad.' He continued. 'Albert had finished his dinner and was putting on his corporal's uniform when the telephone rang. According to his wife Mary the caller who, she assumed from the conversation he knew, had broken down at the bottom of Corkscrew Hill between Tiddledurn and Melbury. Later she told the police he wasn't happy at being late for the parade but couldn't leave someone stranded, so he drove back to the garage to collect his tow truck.

'Just after ten o'clock that night when he hadn't returned home Mary rang Captain William Howe, the commanding Officer of the Home Guard. He confirmed to her that Albert had never arrived, which was surprising as he never missed a parade. She told him about the earlier phone call. Howe, a former officer in the regular army, said he would drive to the garage. Before leaving home, he phoned his platoon sergeant at the lock cottage.

Zed thought for a moment. 'What here?'

Tim smiled. 'Yes, it was my grandfather.' Darkness had crept unnoticed into the room. Peggy turned on the lights and drew the curtains across the old sash windows. Tim drained the last of his whisky-laced tea from his cup.

'When both men arrived at the garage in the village it was in darkness. The front and rear doors were locked. The breakdown truck was missing from the forecourt and Albert's car was parked in its place, so they headed towards Corkscrew Hill. The lanes were dark and a heavy drizzle more than occupied the wipers. About a mile from the hill they came to a crossroads. My grandfather's platoon had been there only two days before, removing all the signposts in the area in case Hitler invaded.'

Dwain said, 'But they wouldn't have been able to read English.'

Tim laughed. 'Good point lad, but Winston Churchill had other ideas.' He massaged his droopy moustache for what seemed an age. 'At the side of the road the gib of the lone breakdown truck was silhouetted against the moon's light, its hook hanging menacingly from a long chain. Captain Howe had taken the precaution of bringing his revolver with him and feeling unease in his gut drew it before both men approached the parked vehicle.'

'Where was the broken down car?' asked Dwain.

Tim shrugged. 'There wasn't one.'

Betty, who was as enthralled with the story as the boys, asked, 'What about Albert Cook?'

Tim shook his head. 'No sign of him. There was though a patch of blood and scuff marks on the ground next to the open driver's door.'

'As if he'd been dragged out?' said Zed

Tim shrugged. 'Possibly. Anyway my grandfather stayed with the truck while Captain Howe drove to the nearest phone box to call the police. There were searches and an investigation for weeks afterwards but, without a body or any other evidence, the case was eventually wound down. Of course, there were numerous conspiracy theories at the time, but nobody really took them seriously. It seemed he had just disappeared from the face of the earth.'

Peggy yawned. 'I think that's enough for tonight boys. It's getting late. You have school tomorrow, and I need to walk your gran back home.'
They both groaned loudly. 'No, not again,' cried Zed, 'we're nearly at the end.'
Betty laughed, 'Something to look forward to tomorrow.'

Tim stood up. 'Peg's right boys. Come on, I'll walk back to Turtle with you.'

# CHAPTER EIGHTEEN

## When One Door Closes

The following morning, the teenage zombies, as Tim had called Zed and Dwain, sleepily gulped down bowls of corn flakes before staggering out of the door to catch the school bus in Tiddledurn village. Tim was enjoying his second brew of the day when his phone rang; it was Harry's niece. She had been to visit him in hospital. He was recovering well but was anxious to see Tim.

Peggy asked, 'Do you think it's to do with the marina?'

Tim shrugged. 'No idea, though it wouldn't surprise me.'

She put two plates of egg and bacon on the table. 'Maybe he's thinking of selling it.'

'Very likely, in the circumstances. It'll be many a month before he can return to work there, and what happens in the meantime?' Before eating he poured water into a glass and swallowed two pain killers.

Peggy sighed with exasperation. 'You can't keep taking those things. Make an appointment to see someone about your back.'

He nodded. 'I will when I have time.'

'Make time,' she replied firmly.

Built in the 1960's Melbury General Hospital sat like a red bricked blob on the outskirts of the town. After circumnavigating the sprawling car park, Tim eventually managed to find a space for the Land Rover, although his blood pressure rose rapidly when he saw the expensive charges. The Cardiac Unit was on the second floor. Harry was in one of four beds occupying a small ward.

Tim was shocked at his friend's pale, drawn features, but still said, 'Hello mate, you're looking better.'

Harry half smiled, ignoring Tim's attempt at deception, albeit well meaning. 'Good to see you Tim, I say good to see you.'

Tim gently took Harry's limp hand then sat in a bedside chair. 'I came as soon as I could.'

Harry smiled. 'I know, after the operation I was in ICU for a time, apparently it was touch and go, I say touch and go.'

Tim stayed for an hour. In between their conversations Harry would occasionally drift off in mid sentence, then wake apologetically and continue, often not where he had left off; all this, against a background of soft moans from an adjoining bed, muffled noises, and the repetitive bleeping of monitoring machines. The nurses, like extras in a silent movie shuffled efficiently across the highly polished floor. It was the smell though, a mixture of over boiled cabbage and antiseptic which always reminded him why he hated hospitals.

Before Tim left him, Harry opened his pyjama jacket to reveal a vivid red, pencil-thin scar stretching from chest bone to navel. He chuckled. 'No quick way back from this I'm afraid, I say no quick way back.'

Tim was surprised by the extent of the invasive surgery. He put his hand tenderly on Harry's shoulder. 'I'll give great thought to what we've discussed. Now you just concentrate on getting better, and don't worry about it.'

Harry smiled. 'That's all I ask, I say, that's all I ask.'

Tim didn't drive directly to the marina, instead stopping off at Bluebell Wood. It had once been a favourite haunt to walk Barney who loved chasing sticks along the shallow stream. The small refreshment hut had re-opened after Easter. He ordered a mug of tea and an Eccles cake then sat down at one of the picnic benches. Harry's words had taken him completely by surprise and he needed time and space to consider the enormity of the proposal.

A green mini bus belonging to Tiddledurn Junior School pulled in on the opposite side of the car park. Doors opened and eager young children tumbled out holding jam jars and fishing nets. He waved to Janice Phillips the Headteacher. It brought back memories of when he and Peggy had first met Zed after he had stowed away on the narrowboat. It was Janice who had visited his grandmother in Rotherhithe and from whose home he would later abscond on the eve of being returned to London.

He ordered another tea from the chatty woman in the red and white striped apron.
Fingers of sunlight pierced the abundant spring foliage of the surrounding trees, birds bickering in their heights. Arm in arm elderly couples nodded a greeting as they passed by on their morning walk. A group of young mothers, all with smart push chairs, emerged from a footpath, their loud youthful laughter providing an antidote to Tim's conflicted mind.

Among the many dog walkers, he recognised a few who used to play with Barney. He used to get on well with most other breeds, but not Boxers. Tim never did work out why. He checked his watch. There was no desire to move from this meditative place, but Jackdaw's engine would not replace itself.

As he stood to go, the dull pain in his lower back made him wince. Waving goodbye to the woman in the red and white striped apron he clambered aboard the Land Rover and drove out of the car park.

Fortunately, Jackdaw was moored close to the service jetty. Tim drew alongside the water's edge and turned off the Land Rover's engine. Across the marina the burnt out hull was still secured to the charred pontoon, its blackened supports rising above the waterline like rows of rotten teeth. The police and fire investigators had finished their work and the blue and white crime scene tape had been removed.

Days earlier he had erected a cradle over the stern end of Jackdaw so the engine could be removed safely. He dropped the tailboard of the Land Rover, gripped the handle of his toolbox, and lifted. A bolt of pain coursed through his body reverberating in every limb. He staggered backwards leaning against the Land Rover for support. Breathing deeply, he waited for the worst of the spasms to pass before slowly walking back to the office. Taking two pain killers he carefully eased himself into Harry's battered leather chair and closed his eyes.

Peggy was angry. She had phoned to see how his visit to Harry had gone. Clearly from his voice he was in pain. 'Have you phoned the doctor?'

He mumbled something about it will pass.

She bit like an African crocodile. 'Right, I'm calling the surgery now.'

The phone went dead. Looking out across the sleepy marina, ripples of water glinting silver against the moored boats, he wondered if fate had played a part in recent events.

Though he hadn't mentioned it to anyone else, he had realised for some time that his ability to continue doing heavy work was waning fast and his back pain reinforced that. Maybe Harry's offer had come at the right time. The desk phone rang. It was Peggy. 'Ten o'clock tomorrow with Doctor Bradley. Now stop what you are doing and come home and rest.'

He did as she asked without argument.

When Peggy responded to the doorbell, she was surprised to see Rocket Ron standing there clutching a coloured folder. Stepping inside he was equally surprised to see Tim sprawled out on the sofa. He chuckled. 'You skiving mate?'

Tim groaned. 'I wish. The old back's giving me a problem.'

'How's things with you Ron?' asked Peggy. 'I hear Rose is thinking of moving into one of those sheltered housing places in Melbury.'

Ron shook his head. 'She seems pretty set on the idea. I'm going to look at one with her on Monday.'

'They're not cheap to buy,' observed Tim.

'I know, but she has the treasure which old Mr Coote left her and the money she gets from the sale of the boat.'

'And what about you?' asked Peggy.

He sat down in one of the chairs by the dining table. 'Frankly I'm devastated. I shall miss her more than I care to admit, but all that matters is what's best for her.'

Tim shifted his position in a half hearted attempt to get up. 'Now I would offer to make a brew but.......'

Peggy raised her eyes. 'Tea or coffee Ron?'

Laughing, he replied, 'Tea. Thanks Peggy.'

Tim laid his head back on the cushion. 'So, what brings you over Ron?'

He tapped the folder on the table. 'This, the Daisy Kearns disappearance case.'

Tim chuckled. 'You still working on that mate?'

He nodded. 'I am indeed and making progress, but I need yours and Peg's historical knowledge.

Tim laughed. 'Blimey, how old do you think we are?'

Peggy brought in a tray of tea and biscuits then sat down next to Ron. 'I overheard what you were saying to Tim. It sounds interesting.'

Ron opened the folder and spread the contents out on the table. 'It is interesting Peg, most interesting.'

Like Rose before her, Peggy was initially startled by the **TOP SECRET** header. Again, Ron explained how the documents had been obtained by a contact of Sharon Giddings, the editor of the Melbury Echo.

Tim said, 'Sounds a bit cloak and dagger to me.'

Ron smiled. 'I think that's exactly what it is or was.' Placing the faded photograph and map of Tiddledurn together, he pointed to the red circle marked Ivy House. 'Do you recognise this location?' he asked.

For a few minutes Peggy looked closely at the black and white copies. 'There used to be a private school on the outskirts of the village. It closed in the 1970's. I can't be sure it's that though.'

Tim eased himself up on the sofa. 'Let me have a look.'

Ron scooped up the documents and passed them to him. He took a pair of reading glasses from his pocket and perched them on the end of his nose.

Peggy laughed. 'Makes him look like an old owl.'

After a few moments of silent observation, Tim said. 'You're right Peg. Those were the gates to Marshdean Preparatory School. It was a big old rambling place. We played a couple of football matches against them when I was at junior school.'

'Is it still there?' Ron asked eagerly.

Tim beckoned him over. Putting the photo aside he picked up the map, then pointing to the crossroads said, 'One of those junctions now leads into the Ramsden Housing Estate which was built in the 1980s. Along with an old mill, Marshdean School was demolished to make way for that.'

Slightly disappointed, Ron asked, 'So would you say this was the correct location?'

Tim nodded. 'I think it is my friend. From this, it looks very much as if Marshdean School was called Ivy House before and possibly during the war.'

Ron chuckled to himself. 'That's very intriguing.'

'What do the other two documents say?' Peggy asked.

Ron turned to the grainy printed text on each sheet. Within certain paragraphs on the pages, he had highlighted those areas of interest which he felt might help place more of the jigsaw pieces together. He passed one of them to Tim.

'This is where it gets very interesting.'

Tim took it and replaced his glasses.

## MINISTRY OF WAR – WHITEHALL OCTOBER 1940
### Military Operation Green Fields - Location Restricted
### Intelligence - Communication
### Code Name – 'FRANCOIS'

Tim read it through again. 'Sorry Ron, am I missing something here?'

'I know it seems like that at first. But remember these two written sheets were deliberately attached to the map and photo, which highlighted the location of Ivy House.'

Tim thought for a moment. 'So, you think Ivy House, formally Marshdean School was the site of this Operation Green Fields, whatever that was?'

Ron nodded. 'I do.'

Tim tapped the document. 'What's Francois?'

'You have to view the words Intelligence and Communication in relation to FRANCOIS, which I discovered was the British code word for the French Resistance.'

Peggy, who had been listening carefully, said, 'So, Operation Green Fields could have been a receiving station for incoming French Resistance Intelligence.'

'That's it exactly,' said Ron.

Tim chuckled. 'Assuming all this is true, and who am I to question the Rocket Ron Detective Agency, what has it to do with the disappearance of Daisy Kearns?' Ron tapped his nose. 'Now my dear Watson, we come to the 'pièce de résistance' of the case.'

# CHAPTER NINETEEN

## The British Traitor

Ron pushed the remaining document across the table towards Peggy. 'Would you mind reading the highlighted items aloud?' he asked, like a provincial lawyer conducting a cross examination in court. She cleared her throat.

*SPECIAL OPERATIONS EXECUTIVE ( S.O.E)*
*TOP SECRET – ACCESS RESTRICTED – February 1942*
*OPERATION GREEN FIELDS*
*'FRANCOIS' - Inbound communication - Compromised Installation 'Dennis' March 1942*

Peggy took a deep breath. Ron smiled as he watched her little cogs turning. 'Someone was attempting to intercept messages being sent to us by the French Resistance?'

'Not just someone,' Ron replied, 'but as I believe, a British traitor spying for the Germans.'
Tim, who was still lying prone on the sofa, asked to see the document. He read through it again. 'I still don't see the connection with Daisy Kearns.'
Ron leant over his shoulder and pointed to the highlighted text.

'We know that Dennis was the code name for a British agent. The document refers to such a person being 'installed' in March 1942, whose mission was to locate the infiltrator. This corresponds with her arrival as a Land Army girl at Muckle Farm. But it was a cover identity. I'm sure that Daisy Kearns was Dennis.

As I thought earlier; why would an obviously intelligent young woman, working in a radar station in Kent, suddenly transfer to the Land Army to pick potatoes down here in Tiddledurn? Don't forget there are also the missing five months of her service record.'

'So where do you think she was then?' asked Tim.

'Training with the SOE before being sent down here.'

Tim stretched. 'Well, you certainly have a vivid imagination Ron.'

Peggy didn't agree with his cynicism.

'If Daisy Kearns was Dennis, she may have discovered the identity of the traitor,' Ron added.

'And what if they realised their cover had been blown? That would have put her in great danger,' Peggy continued. 'She would need to be stopped before reporting back to the SOE.'

Ron nodded. 'And that's what I believe happened to Daisy Kearns.'

Tim shifted to a more comfortable position on the sofa.

'But no body was ever found,' said Peggy. 'It would have been easy to dispose of one, particularly in war time. And what about Albert Cook? He disappeared earlier; doesn't that strike you as odd?'

Tim shrugged. 'Probably a coincidence.'

She stood up from the table. 'I doubt after all this time we'll ever really know what happened to her, but I think you've done well Ron piecing all this together. It's fascinating.'

He slid the documents back into the folder. 'Thanks Peg. I'm going to see Sharon Giddings at the Echo next week. She said they might be interested in doing an article on it.'

'Oh, that would be wonderful. It's a good story,' said Peggy.

'Now I'd better get going or Frankie and Freddie will be driving Rose round the bend.'

Tim asked, 'How are the little furry creatures?'

'Oh, they're alright. At least I'll have them for company when Rose moves on.'

Peggy smiled sympathetically. 'You know we're here for you anytime Ron.'

As he crossed the lawn she called after him. 'Give my love to Rose.' He turned and waved.

Tim eased himself up into a sitting position. 'He's going to miss her.'

Peggy agreed. 'Such a shame. It worries me him being moored all alone at Muckle Farm. Now I'll put the kettle on, and you can tell me all about your visit with Harry.'

Later that afternoon the school bus pulled alongside the kerb in Tiddledurn village. Earlier, when boarding outside Melbury Comprehensive, the youngsters had breathed a sigh of relief. The normal irritating driver with his inane comments had been replaced by a friendly young woman. Those getting off outside the Post Office stood in small groups talking with their friends and checking their phones, before walking off in different directions.

As usual, Lady Barrington Gore was waiting across the road in her green Range Rover. Phoebe, aware of her mother's hawkish eyes quickly pulled Dwain behind the telephone box for a long goodbye kiss. George and Zed weren't being so bold. In George, Zed had found a soulmate who shared his sensitivities and interests. Although the same age, there was a greater maturity in George's character.

Of course, Zed's affection for Dwain was undiminished, but that was as a brother's love and siblings, no matter how close, often have different personalities and outlooks. Zed and George though were aware of anxieties bubbling beneath the surface of their friendship as they covertly navigated their sexual attraction to each other. How they envied the ease with which Dwain and Phoebe, and other friends, outwardly demonstrated their teenage crushes. George glanced across to his waiting mother before moving close to Zed and squeezing his hand. Before he could respond there was a loud hooting from an impatient Lady Barrington Gore. 'Come on George, we have to go,' called Phoebe.

Since Peggy had moved out to live with Tim, Zed's gran, Betty, had made the small furnished flat above the butcher's shop in Tiddledurn her own. After school, unless Betty was already at the lock side cottage with Tim and Peggy, Zed and Dwain would always call in to see her.

The butcher, Mr Strout, a jolly, rotund man with ruby red cheeks and large hands to match, was standing outside his shop. 'You going to visit that lovely gran of yours, are you?' He winked. Politely smiling at him, Zed rang the bell. Moments later Betty opened the door. As they followed her up the narrow carpeted staircase, Zed said, 'I think Mr Strout fancies you, Gran.'

She laughed heartily at the absurd suggestion. 'Good grief boy, I'm fed up not hard up, and anyway he's married.'

After what she had been through lately Zed loved to hear her laughing again.

The boys sat down on the sofa in the cosy sitting room overlooking the church spire. On a small side table Betty put a plate of freshly made doughnuts oozing with jam. She asked how their day at school had been. 'Alright,' Dwain mumbled. The truth was that they couldn't wait to leave the place and start their Marine Engineering course at Melbury Further Education college.

Betty passed Zed a brown envelope. 'Good news.'
Inside was a letter with a cheque attached. 'Wow,' he exclaimed loudly noting the amount. 'What's it for?'

'It's the insurance pay out for the contents on the flat.'

'That's great Gran, no more charity shops for us then.' She envied his youthful ability to see the picture as it is, rather than was. But she still mourned daily the many personal possessions and mementoes which no amount of insurance money could ever replace. Now only her memory bore testament to a life lived before the London fire. She often reflected on how her life had changed and occasionally missed the bustle of London and her fussing neighbour, Doris. It was, after all, where she had been born and bred and lived all her life. But she was slowly adapting to this peaceful rural existence and Zed continued to thrive on the country air. He would never contemplate moving back. She asked Dwain if he had spoken to his mum in London recently.

'Yeah, last week. They're cool, but it sounds as chaotic as ever. My sister's got a new boyfriend and he's moved in with them.' He chuckled. 'She'll be preggers again soon.'

Betty looked aghast. 'Oh, I do hope not, poor girl.'

Dwain removed his blazer and tie. 'I'm just glad I'm down here and not living in Lewisham with them.'

Betty touched him fondly on the arm. 'So are we love. Now you two eat up and I'll fetch some drinks.'

The church clock struck six as the boys left the flat to walk back to the cottage, leaving the empty doughnut plate behind them. Betty waved from upstairs as they crossed the High Street towards the village green.

Mr Strout was unloading some meat from his van. Looking up at her he raised his straw boater and smiled, his veined florid cheeks glowing like cherry tomatoes. Remembering Zed's earlier remarks, Betty quickly stepped back from the window.

The late afternoon was warm, and the village green buzzed with activity. Sauntering casually, their blazers and bags slung across their shoulders, Zed and Dwain stopped momentarily to watch four men dressed in cricket whites practicing in the nets. Small children floated toy boats on the duck pond watched from surrounding benches by young mothers and elderly folk, no doubt reminiscing on past times. Off the lead dogs chased balls across the short grass, other owners held theirs close as if fearing any canine interaction with other breeds. Whoops of delight came from the adventure playground where, like swarms of ants, youngsters crawled all over the creaking apparatus. Overhead could be heard the throaty growl of a micro light as it travelled from East to West. On the opposite side of the green, where the path met the road, musical chimes from an ice cream van were attracting a sizeable queue. Zed and Dwain were tempted but knew dinner would be ready soon.

Peggy and Tim were in deep discussion when the boys bowled noisily through the door. Tim was sitting on the sofa supported by two large cushions. 'You alright?' Zed asked.

'I am lad, though my back's not.'

Zed sat down next to him. 'What's happened then?'

Tim smiled. 'Nothing's happened. It's just wear and tear I'm afraid?'

Dwain asked, 'Did you see Harry at the hospital?'

Tim nodded. 'I did, and that's what we want to talk to you both about after dinner.'

With a tone of disappointment Zed said, 'I thought we were going to hear the last bit about Wilf Barrington Gore.'

Peggy eased herself up out of the low armchair. 'This is more important love. Now you two get on with your homework and I'll put the dinner on.'

Tim took his phone from his pocket and checked his messages. He was waiting for a reply from his friend 'Chip' Chester, who managed the Brentford Narrowboat Project on the Grand Union Canal. Zed and Dwain spread their homework out across the table. Zed was more compliant in undertaking this nightly task; Dwain viewed it as a waste of time and energy. He studied one paper and huffed. 'Why do I need to know how many trees are felled each year in the Brazilian rain forest?'

Zed laughed. 'It's all to do with global warming dude.'

Dwain sighed in despair. 'Yeah, whatever man.'

# CHAPTER TWENTY
## The Wanderer

Smokey Joe woke early in the caravan at Old Moor Lock. He always did. Rain pattered on the flat roof, the sound muffled by a growing accumulation of soggy moss. He pulled back the curtains to reveal a stubborn darkness delaying the onset of dawn. Blinking away the heavy fog of sleep he lay still, listening to the songbird's morning chorus. He could identify most of the bird calls and did a passable impersonation of some. This he had learnt as a youngster after spending many hours alongside his uncle in the hide at Coote's Wood.

Stepping from the bed he stood momentarily in front of the cracked mirror, which distorted his already strained features. On his right shoulder a jagged purple scar, inflicted by a piece of shrapnel whilst serving with the army in the Iraq war. His mates, closer to the exploding car bomb had not been so fortunate. He saw their youthful faces every day. Throwing on a worn dressing gown he went along the short passage into the chilly silent lounge.

Driftwood's ashes sat alongside his red bowler hat on a shelf. Smokey tapped the top of the plastic urn as he passed. 'Morning, me old mate.' Most days he could almost hear him reply, 'Allo mush.' But not today. He was probably annoyed that Smokey had decided against moving into the cottage at Coote's Wood. The mug of tea and two slices of toast with jam were consumed sitting at the small table overlooking the clearing in front of the caravan.

Overnight rain had blotched the coarse grass with shallow puddles. He smiled as a grey squirrel jumped on top of Driftwood's old pram and stared inquisitively at him through the window. Yawning, he contemplated the forthcoming day. Ben, the carpenter and his partner Remi, had been intrigued when he had asked them to meet him at the cottage in Coote's Wood at eleven o'clock that morning. He washed, combed the knots from his straggly beard, dressed in his now uniformed attire then put on his long ex-army greatcoat secured around the middle with string. Before leaving the caravan, he placed his wide brimmed hat with pheasant's feather on his head. 'See you later Driftwood,' he called as he closed the door behind him.

He checked his watch. At a good pace it should take him no more than forty five minutes to reach Coote's Wood. That was providing he didn't stop to talk to someone, which was highly likely as he knew most people on the cut. The towpath was very familiar to him as it hugged the route of the canal, though he never tired of the changing landscape and its many sounds and smells. The seasons always enthralled him, each arriving with their own storyline and unique backdrop. Nature's theatrical performance at its finest, he often thought, though sadly unseen by many as they hurried blindly through their busy day.

A scattering of narrowboats chugged lazily along the still waterway. People working boats through locks exchanged pleasantries as Smokey wandered by, though his odd, unconventional appearance often prompted remarks from children whose embarrassed parents quickly turned them away. He smiled, having heard it all before.

At Farmer's Bridge, where the Melbury road crossed the canal, he climbed up the grass bank then sat on a low wall looking across the fields towards

Tiddledurn and its church spire. Beyond the sharp bend, a signpost stood in the middle of a forked junction, its long white fingers tempting the adventurous traveller with new destinations to explore. It reminded him of the words of his maternal grandmother before he had left to join the army. 'You were born under a wandering star my boy.' At the time he was unsure of the meaning, but now he knew. There are those who settle down and easily find their niche in life, and others for whom the distant horizon is always beyond reach.

Part way along a straight stretch of path, where the power cables hummed overhead, Smokey could see Ben and Remi waiting by the gate which led into Coote's Wood and the cottage beyond. Their small black spaniel, whose name Smokey had forgotten, came running towards him yapping loudly. Bending down he stroked its floppy ears.

'He remembered you,' said Remi.

Smokey chuckled. 'More like the smell of the rabbits I brought you last time.'

Ben asked, 'So, what's this all about then mate?' Smokey removed the padlock from the gate. 'Come in and all will be revealed.'

Remi chuckled. 'Sounds very exciting.'

They walked along the tree lined gravel track until they reached the small unkept garden in front of the renovated cottage. The little spaniel lay on the grass chewing a large stick. Pointing to the new veranda Ben asked proudly. 'What do you think of that Rem, all my own work?'

The recently constructed cedar wood structure stretched full width across the front of the white painted facia. Three wooden steps led up from the path towards the double doors. Shards of sunlight glinted off the glossy varnished surface. Remi was impressed.

'Wow, that's really nice Ben.'

Smokey added. 'Yeah, he's a clever lad.' Fishing deep into the pocket of the army greatcoat he pulled out a set of keys. 'I hope you will both enjoy sitting out here on summer's evenings.'

Ben and Remi exchanged a quizzical look at each other. Then Ben said, 'Sorry mate, I'm not with you.'

Smokey beckoned them to sit down on the wooden seat opposite the weathered bird bath. The stunned couple became increasingly motionless as for the next ten minutes Smokey outlined his proposal. Then with the casualness of a man liberated, he finished and sat down on the grass. At first no words were spoken. The silence being broken only by the rustling trees. Remi took Ben's hand, a small tear wetting her pink cheek.  Feeling as if the earth had shifted beneath him Ben asked emotionally, 'You would do this for us Smokey?'

He laughed and threw Ben the keys. 'Why not, you need somewhere to live and bring up that child of yours safely, and this neglected old house needs to be a home again.'

'But what about you?' asked Remi.

Smokey beamed. 'Oh, I'll be fine. I have my freedom back and now we can go wandering again.' Ben looked confused.

'Whose we?'

Smokey beamed. 'Me and my old mate Driftwood, men of the road.'

Remi put her arms around him and kissed him on the cheek. He blushed.

Smokey Joe wasn't the only one pulling surprises from the hat. After dinner the previous evening Zed and Dwain had sat dumbstruck as Peggy and Tim spoke to them. It is often assumed that it is only the elderly who are fazed by change, but the same can be attributed to youngsters when the stability of their lives seems suddenly threatened. Peggy and Tim understood this and were careful how they framed this conversation.

Tim explained that even before the heart attack, Harry had been considering selling the marina as it was getting too much for him to manage. But he didn't want it to fall into the hands of a big company and lose its personal touch.

'Anyway, when I went to visit him in hospital, he made me an offer,' said Tim.

Dwain interjected, 'You're going to buy it?'

Tim laughed. 'What makes you think I can afford that?'

Dwain shrugged. 'Dunno, depends how much it is?'

Peggy smiled. 'A lot of money love.'

Tim paused. 'There is another way though. Harry has offered us a long term lease.'

Zed asked, 'What does that mean?'

Peggy answered. 'It's a type of contract between Harry and us. He would retain ownership of the marina and receive an annual percentage of the income, but we would run it on a day to day basis.'

Not fully grasping the implications the boys were a little underwhelmed by the suggestion.

'Sounds cool to me,' said Zed. 'We could help out too.'

Tim ran his fingers slowly through his droopy moustache. Then choosing his words carefully said,

'But if we take it on there will have to be changes.' The word bit into their flesh.

'What changes?' Zed asked abruptly.

'Well, for one, I will have to give up maintaining boats on the canal, which the way my back is at present will be a blessing.'

'But what about all your customers?' asked Zed.

Tim shrugged. 'There are others out there who will do the work short term.' He winked at Peggy, but neither of the boys picked up on the expression 'short term.'

Looking anxious Dwain asked, 'Does this mean we won't be going to college when we leave school?'

Tim laughed. 'Of course not. You will attend your day release course at the college, as planned, working the remainder of the week with me, where I can teach you the rest.

Confused, Zed asked. 'But I thought...........?'

Tim anticipated the question. 'I said that I wouldn't be maintaining boats on the canal anymore, not the marina. But I'm going to need two strong apprentices to help me do that.'

Peggy continued, 'The idea is that eventually, when you are qualified, all the maintenance work in the marina, and anything coming in from the canal will be yours. That will provide you with a secure future.' She paused. 'So, what do you think of the plan so far?'

'It's brill,' Zed answered.

Smiling broadly, Dwain said, 'It's cool by me.' But reflecting on the word 'changes' plural, asked suspiciously, 'What else then?'

'Well,' said Peggy, 'as you know there haven't been many bookings lately for Odin and Thor.

Many of the organisations we used to carry no longer have the budget. Which means, with the towpath moorings, insurance and licence costs it's no longer viable to operate the boats. And even if it were, we wouldn't have time to crew them.'

Although they had discussed it beforehand, Peggy's brisk assessment of the situation struck sadness in even Tim's pragmatic heart. His mind drifted back to twenty five years ago when he had first acquired the two ex-working boats. The idea originally was to convert Odin, the one with the engine, and sell it on, keeping Thor, the butty, for storage. It was Peggy, who he had known since childhood, who had suggested turning them into residential trip boats. She had recently taken youngsters from Tiddledurn Youth Club to a similar project on the Grand Union Canal and had been impressed by how much they had enjoyed it and learned about the waterways.

Zed, stung by the implied suggestion, reacted indignantly. 'You're not thinking of selling them? You can't do that!'

Before Tim could answer him, Dwain said, 'We could crew 'em at weekends and during the holidays.'

Zed nodded. 'Yeah, you said we were old enough to handle them now.'

Tim studied their bewildered faces. He knew they had both spent too many happy and formulative times onboard for it to be an agreeable decision. For Zed it was a particular blow. Odin and Thor had been as much an intrinsic part of his new-found life, as Tim, Peggy, Barney and all the other characters he had met since fate deposited him in Tiddledurn.

Tim replied gently. 'We know you can handle the boats and did consider that possibility.

Had it been one or two years ahead it may have been an option, but you are still at school, then you have your Marine Engineering qualification course which will be hard work.' He chuckled. 'And you will need some time to yourselves. All work and no play, makes Jack a dull boy.' Zed was tempted to ask who Jack was but didn't.

'You do understand the situation boys, don't you?' asked Peggy.

There was a moment's sullen silence before they reluctantly nodded their agreement.

# CHAPTER TWENTY ONE

## Amos Buck

The cuckoo clock struck eight. Peggy looked up at the irritating squawking bird.

'Who fancies a drink then?'

Tim chuckled. 'Silly question, Peg.' He never refused a brew, and both the boys were addicted to her recipe for hot chocolate drinks. Repositioning the cushions supporting his painful back, Tim asked, 'So how are you two managing on Turtle?'

Surprised by the randomness of the question, Zed said, 'Alright. Why?'

Dwain hesitated before answering, then tentatively replied, 'Well I suppose, I mean, as we're getting older............?'

Tim interrupted him. 'You could do with a bit more space of your own?'

Looking apprehensively at Zed, Dwain nodded. 'Yeah.'

Tim asked, 'What about you Zed?'

He shrugged indifferently. 'S'pose, it makes sense.'

Smiling, Tim said, 'Thought I'd just ask.'

From the kitchen Peggy had heard every word of his probing question and knew the reason for asking it. She placed a tray with brimming mugs and slices of homemade Victoria sponge on the table. 'Right, meeting's over. Help yourselves.'

Tim gave a pained expression as he attempted to stand up from the sofa. Peggy shook her head in despair. 'Will somebody please put him out of his misery.'

The boys laughed as they handed him his tea and cake. Sitting down in the low armchair she told the boys about Rocket Ron's earlier visit. Zed asked Peggy how he was. 'Excited; he thinks he's solved the mystery of the Daisy Kearns case.'

Licking the jam from his lips Dwain asked, 'Is that the Land Army girl who went missing?'

Peggy nodded. 'That's right love, during the war in 1943.'

Tim chuckled. 'According to the Rocket Ron Detective Agency, she was really a secret British agent.

Zed laughed. 'What in Tiddledurn?'

Tim shrugged. 'Apparently so. There was a Top Secret Instillation which this informant was tasked with extracting classified information from, then sending it back to Germany.'

'So, what does he think happened to her then?'

'Ron's theory is that she discovered this person's identity. Knowing his cover was blown and fearing exposure and arrest............

Dwain interrupted him. 'He topped 'er.'

Zed's eyes brightened. 'This is cool man, a real live British traitor here. I wonder how he did it, probably a Luger. All the Germans used Lugers. I've seen it on TV.'

Tim said. 'We don't know he was German.'

Dwain shook his head. 'No, that's too messy dude, a cheese wire would be quieter.' He made a garrotting movement with his hands. Zed added, 'Or forced her to swallow a cyanide pill. All the agents carried those in case of being captured and interrogated.'

Peggy had heard enough of this macabre discussion. 'You two certainly have a good imagination.'

'Well, whatever happened to the poor girl, they never found her,' said Tim.

Dwain asked, 'There was that other bloke who went missing too?'

Peggy answered, 'Yes, Albert Cook. That was before Daisy Kearns, and he was never seen again.'

Zed shook his head. 'That's weird man. It could have been Aliens snatching people to do experiments on their bodies. I read about that happening somewhere.'

Peggy laughed. 'I don't think it had anything to do with little green men in spaceships love.'

Then unexpectedly Dwain said, 'How about Wilf?'

'What do you mean?' Peggy asked.

'Well, you said Albert Cook had threatened to kill Wilf him for getting his daughter preggers. Maybe he got there first.'

Zed thought for a moment. 'Yeah, but why would he? And anyway, he was still in Germany.'

Tim paused briefly as he reflected on his grandfather telling him the same story all those years ago. 'Actually, Wilf did come back, at least according to Old Amos Buck.'

Peggy chuckled, 'Not that anyone believed him at the time.'

'Why not?' asked Zed.

Tim tapped the whisky bottle which was standing on a table next to the sofa. 'The demon drink. Amos did enjoy a tipple, or two.'

Peggy added, 'He was the local poacher, a strange unkept looking character.' She smiled. 'He didn't look dissimilar to poor old Driftwood. When us school girls used to see him coming in the village, we'd cross over the road to avoid him.' Chuckling, she continued, 'He did pong a bit, though he was an old man by then.'

Tim continued. 'Well according to his story, which he told the following night in the bar of the Red Lion, he had been poaching in Knocker's Wood. It was a favourite haunt of his, being on the boundary of the Barrington Gore Estate and therefore rarely patrolled by its gamekeepers. Carrying his illegal catch in a sack he walked home along the lane which passes by the Manor House. Although dark like pitch, he was careful to stay out of the illuminating eye of the full moon, keeping where possible to the shadows. As he drew near to the gates, a car with dimmed headlights approached from the opposite direction. Fearing it might be the police he hid behind the trunk of a tree. The vehicle, a big black Humber, slowed then stopped. As the driver stepped out to open the gates, a beam of moon light briefly silhouetted the passenger in the rear seat who, according to Amos, was Wilf Barrington Gore.'

Peggy explained. 'To be on the safe side, the landlord reported it to the local police, but generally the villagers discounted it as Wilf was never seen around Tiddledurn. Although with the blackouts it would have been easy for someone to move around the area undetected.'

Tim yawned. 'So that's as much as we know about the Barrington Gores, and the sightings and movements of Wilf remain forever unsolved.'

It was ten o'clock when Zed and Dwain reluctantly left the cottage to walk back to spend the night on Turtle.

Afterwards Peggy asked, 'So, what are you contemplating about the boy's future accommodation?'

Tim poured himself a large glass of malt whisky. 'Well, it seems we have two options. Both Ben and Rose's boats will be coming up for sale. Once Odin and Thor are moved, we could moor whichever one in front of Turtle.'

Peggy added, 'Giving them both a boat each.'

Tim nodded. 'Exactly Peg.'

She smiled. I think Ben and Remi's boat would be better for them, it's a more spacious modern interior.'

Tim took another drink, swirling it slowly around his mouth as he savoured the rich, velvety, peaty taste. 'After Rose has moved into her sheltered housing, we could offer Rocket Ron a mooring as well. That way he would be near the boys and us if anything happened and wouldn't be stuck at Muckle Farm on his own. What do you think Peg?'

She beamed at his thoughtfulness. 'It's a great idea. I think he'll jump at it.'

Tim chuckled. 'You never know, he can be an independent old devil.'

Peggy winked. 'I'll work on him.'

For a time, they sat in silence with just the standard lamp throwing a yellow glow into the small cosy room. Peggy lit a candle. It flickered, casting ghostly shadows off the white walls. Outside, the only sound was an intermittent hoot from a barn owl. Peggy sat next to Tim on the sofa and held his leathery hand. 'No regrets?' she asked.

He turned to look at her. Wisps of grey were now appearing in her once mousy hair, though the hue of her weathered complexion was still as radiant as ever. He smiled. 'How could I have? Who'd have thought at our time of life we would have an oven-ready family around us!'

Before going to sleep on Turtle that night Dwain stood over Zed bashing him remorselessly with a pillow. 'I told Tim, it would be a good idea for us both to have some more space, not that I didn't want to live here with you anymore.'

Laughing and fending off the soft blows Zed shouted, 'Alright man, stop. Stop. I only asked you a question.'

Tired, they both collapsed panting on the bed. Before climbing into their sleeping bags Dwain said, 'Anyway dude, there's nowhere else we can go, so we're stuck with each other.'

Zed smiled. 'That's cool by me.'

It had taken three men all day to clear out the old wine cellar beneath the ground floor of the Manor House. Lady Barrington Gore had scrutinised carefully every item being removed, in the expectation that a valuable family heirloom may have been buried amongst the decades of stored junk, but alas it was not to be. With Phoebe and George, she watched as Milo and Morgan the two black Labradors chased the coughing transit van as it drove off along the drive.

Sir Roland Barrington Gore descended the polished wooden staircase into the spacious circular hallway. His dark chiselled features were not dissimilar to the generations of his family whose stern portraits gazed eternally down upon them; the most recent being his father Gerald, Grandfather Morris and Great Uncles Wilf and Edger.

He had not long returned home from his offices in London where he worked three days a week as a metals and grain commodity broker. Dressed in a pair of red chinos and a mustard coloured jersey he clutched the latest copy of the Melbury Echo in his hand. It was not a publication he normally purchased, but an article on the front page had caught his eye.

Outside the front door his wife, Lady Barrington Gore, blew her small metal whistle and Milo and Morgan ran slobbering back along the drive.

'No hidden treasures then?' he asked, smiling.

She shook her head. 'Just junk I'm afraid.' George and Phoebe went along the passage to inspect the now empty cavern. Roland beckoned to his wife. 'I want to show you something.'

She followed him through the double wooden doors into the library. He laid the weekly newspaper on a table and pointed to the secondary headline on the front page.

### EXCLUSIVE
### 'LOCAL MAN'S THEORY ON MISSING LAND ARMY GIRL, DAISY KEARNS'

He pointed. 'Look, it says that during the war there was a Top Secret Instillation based at Marshdean School, which is where my father went.' Lady Barrington Gore, who had married into the family and not being a native of the area, knew little of the mystery which had baffled residents of the village since the war had ended. Sir Roland ran his finger across the third paragraph. 'According to this chap, Ron Hughes, she was murdered by a British traitor, who he thinks was living covertly amongst the local community.'

She gasped. 'But that's awful. I hope they caught him.'

He shrugged. 'Apparently it happened in all the countries across Europe where people who shared the Nazi's ideology wanted them to win the war.'

She read slowly through the article then said light-heartedly. 'You have German descendants, Roland.'

He looked indignant at the inference. 'What on earth do you mean?'
She laughed and touched him on the arm. 'I'm only joking darling. I am sure your family were patriotic to the core.'


Phoebe and George stood on the new staircase leading down into the hollow cavity.
The old wine cellar, which had not been used as such for over seventy years, was completely bare now apart from one length of wooden racking across the far wall. As the others had long since been removed George was confused as to why one had been left in place.
Flakes of ancient paint peeled like skin from the whitewashed walls. A wide spider's web hung abandoned from the blemished ceiling like a seaman's hammock. The generations of previously stored junk had masked a peculiar chilliness which clung to the empty space like a fog.

Lady Barrington Gore appeared suddenly behind them. 'When are you making a start on the decorating?'

Phoebe replied, 'Dwain and Zed are coming over on Saturday.'

She smiled. 'Good, we had better get some materials in then.'

Phoebe and George went out into the passageway. As their mother turned to leave, a movement in the corner caught her eye, then like a flash it was gone. She put out the light and closed the door, dismissing it as a disturbed mouse.

# CHAPTER TWENTY TWO

## The Mystery Caller

Rocket Ron sat at his favourite window seat at The Milan Café off the Market Square in Melbury. Proudly he studied the front page 'Exclusive' printed in the latest edition of the Melbury Echo. Armed with his diligently obtained information the journalist, Adi Adekola, had compiled a detailed story of Land Army girl Daisy Kearns, and the speculative events surrounding her disappearance in 1943.

'Buongiorno, Signor Ron.' He turned. The young daughter of Guiseppe, the Italian owner stood beside him.

'Buongiorno, Sofia. What's that lovely perfume you're wearing?'

She giggled softly. 'Mugler Angel; you like?'

He nodded. 'Yes. I really like it Sofia.' After ordering a latte and a croissant with jam he returned his attention once more to reading the article. The creative licence applied by the scribe had added much more flesh to the bones of his skeletal investigation. There was though, as highlighted by Adi Adekola, one link missing in the chain. What had happened to Albert Cook?'

He took from his pocket a piece of paper which Sharon Giddings had given him earlier that morning. Written on it was a phone number and the name of the caller a Heather Reynolds. She had read the article in the Echo and was keen to speak to Ron rather than the journalist.

The wafting scent of Sofia's 'Mugler Angel' perfume reached him before the arrival of the latte and croissant.

'Buon appetito, Signor Ron.'

'Grazie Sofia, Grazie.' As she turned to go her long black hair swished seductively around her shoulders. Taking a bite from the freshly baked croissant he chuckled at the heart shape Sofia had made on top of his coffee. Over the sound system the 'Love Theme' from the 'Godfather' was playing. He closed his eyes and for some time imagined himself wandering casually with Sofia across the sun drenched Sicilian hills.

'Silly old fool,' he thought to himself. Taking out his phone he tapped in Heather Reynolds' number. It rang for some time before a voice answered. 'Hello, sorry I was in the garden.'

'Hello. My name is Ron Hughes. Sharon Giddings said you wanted to speak to me about the article in the Echo.'

There was a slight pause. In the background he could hear the low rumble of a tumble dryer and the chirping of a caged bird.

Her voice was soft. 'Yes, that's right. Thank you for calling back. I have some information for you about Albert Cook.'

He was at first taken aback at this sudden development, then tentatively asked. 'Why me and not Adi Adekola?'

She laughed. 'You know what journalists are, they'll write anything to sell a story.'

He chuckled. 'This is the Melbury Echo we're talking about, not a Sunday newspaper.'

'I know,' she replied, 'but this information is rather sensitive and not for publication, even after all these years. You'll understand why when we meet.'

Ron was hungrily curious. Who was this woman? And what was her connection to the story?

'Where do you suggest then?' he asked. 'I'm near Tiddledurn, where are you?'

Slightly evasive, she answered. 'Oh, that doesn't matter, I have a car and can travel to you.'

They agreed to meet the following Sunday morning in the tea shop in Tiddledurn High Street.

'Look forward to it,' she said, before disconnecting the call.

Ron sat for a time contemplating the conversation with Heather Reynolds. The circumstances regarding garage owner Albert Cook were certainly sketchy. He had apparently taken a phone call at his home from someone claiming to have broken down at the bottom of Corkscrew Hill between Tiddledurn and Melbury asking him to attend. Much later that night after his wife had raised the alarm, his tow truck had been found abandoned and he was missing.

He finished his croissant and coffee. The café had emptied out with only him and one other customer remaining. Amused, he watched the rotund man, with pronounced sweating jowls, attacking a large bowl of spaghetti bolognaise, occasional splashes of tomato sauce falling onto the white tablecloths.

Sofia was busying herself behind the counter. 'Ah, Signor Ron. Are you leaving us?'

He nodded. 'Afraid so, Sofia. Places to go, people to see.' The truth was just the opposite, he had no desire to return alone to his boat and could quite happily have sat in the comfortable ambiance for the rest of the day. He paid the bill.

'Arrivederci Signor Ron,' Sofia called, as he went out into the market square.

He waved. 'Arrivederci.'

There was a disturbing dullness to his mind which he had never experienced before. It felt as if a heavy weight was pressing down upon his skull. Hoping the fresh air would clear his head, he decided to walk back along the towpath to his moorings at Muckle Farm. Strolling along, his mind drifted back to his friend Rose. He had accompanied her last Monday to view The Orchard sheltered housing complex in Melbury. It was not to his taste, all too neat and sterile, but she had felt comfortable and safe there. He sighed thoughtfully. There was no point in any further discussion, her mind was made up and he resigned himself to being moored forever alone at Muckle Farm.

On Saturday morning Tim stopped the Land Rover on the lane outside the gates to the Manor House, home to the Barrington Gores. Zed said, 'You can go up the driveway.'

Tim shook his head. 'No, I'll drop you here.' Even though Zed and Dwain had struck up a friendship with their children he preferred to keep his distance.

'We'll see you later then,' called Dwain as he and Zed exited the vehicle. Tim tooted the horn as he drove off. They were only part way along the tree lined drive when the two black Labradors, Milo and Morgan, came thundering towards them. Recognising the boys as friends they ceased barking and nudged affectionally against their legs, tails wagging furiously.

Lady Barrington Gore's shrill metal whistle sounded, and the two hounds obediently bounded back towards the house. The boys followed behind.

Phoebe and George's mother was sitting on the front steps drinking from a large red mug.
Dwain whispered. 'Do you reckon she sleeps in that body warmer and green wellies?' Zed giggled.
Hearing their feet on the gravel she looked up. 'Ah, I wondered what the dogs were barking at. Go on through. Phoebe and George are waiting for you in the kitchen.' They crossed the spacious circular entrance hall where portraits of past Barrington Gores stared intensely down upon them.

George jumped up from the kitchen table where he and his sister had been eating breakfast.
'Hey dudes.' He bumped fists with Zed and Dwain. Phoebe was less demonstrative, she smiled sweetly. 'Thanks for coming to play.'

Dwain grinned cheekily. 'What are we playing at then Pheeb?'

She laughed. 'Not what you have in mind.'

'Come on then, let's get started,' George said enthusiastically. They followed him along the passageway which led to the old wine cellar. The door was ajar. George pushed it open and switched on the lights. Zed and Dwain had only ever seen it filled with generations of stored junk. Now in stark contrast it displayed a cold nakedness. The quartet descended the recently fitted stairs and stood in the middle of the empty concrete floor. Zed looked around him. 'So, what do we start on then?'

Phoebe answered him. 'Daddy says painting and decorating is all in the preparation, so we have to wash all the walls down first, then fill any cracks or holes.'

George laughed mockingly. 'I don't know how he would know that, he's never done any repairs.' He pointed at the last remaining wine rack. 'We have to remove that thing first, then we can have a bonfire in the garden.'

Dwain walked over to inspect the wooden structure. It was secured to the wall by four long bolts which passed through the uprights into the brickwork. He shook it. There was no movement.
Turning to the others he said, 'It's pretty solid, we're going to have to force it away from the wall.'
Concerned, Phoebe asked. 'Won't that cause damage?'
He shrugged. 'Probably, but a few bricks and a bit of plaster can be repaired easily afterwards.'

He beckoned them over and pointed to a narrow gap between the shelving and where it buttressed the brickwork. 'If we could get something in there, we should be able to lever it away from the wall.'
George grabbed Zed's arm. 'Come on, let's look in the garden shed, there's bound to be something useful in there.'

Phoebe shouted after them. 'Don't be too long.'

They went back through the kitchen to a door on the far side which led out onto the garden at the rear of the house. The shed stood alongside the lawn and against a tall hedge. It had clearly seen better days. The once treated wood was now dull and cracked. A section of the rain proofed felt had become detached from the roof and flapped about in the breeze.

They went inside the musty smelling small interior, with cluttered shelves on either side. George grinned mischievously. 'Close the door.' As Zed turned, he threw his arms around his neck and kissed him passionately on the lips. Zed at first stiffened at the suddenness of this embrace.

George whispered in his ear. 'Relax dude, it's cool, we're good.'

He did, and taking George around the waist they kissed. He gave a small gasp as he felt George exploring his body. They both stood locked in the moment of their first real intimate encounter. Then like a pin pricking a balloon Lady Barrington Gore called.

'Shit,' George exclaimed loudly.

Zed put a finger across his lips. 'She'll hear you,' he whispered, giggling.

George went outside. His mother was standing at the kitchen door, the two dogs at her feet. 'We're looking for some tools,' he called defensively.

'So Phoebe said. I'm going to Melbury to meet some friends for coffee. There's lunch for you all in the kitchen. Your father should be home from golf before me.'

He waved. 'Ok Ma, see you later.'

When he went back into the shed, Zed had a wide grin on his freckled face. 'That was a close thing man.' With a twinkle in his eye, George said, 'Worth the risk though wasn't it.'

In the cellar Phoebe and Dwain were sitting on the stairs waiting for them. 'Haughtily, she demanded, 'Where have you been?'

Zed was holding a club hammer in his hand, George, a heavy wrench and a long screw driver.

He retorted, 'It took time to find these, you know what a mess it is in that shed.'

Dwain caught Zed's eye and winked. He blushed.

'Right,' said Phoebe jumping up. 'Let's do it.' Being the strongest amongst them, Dwain took the wrench from George.

'So, what shall we do?' asked Zed. Dwain thought for a moment.

'You three take hold of the front of the rack and as I work it loose, pull on it.'

Pushing the flat edge of the heavy wrench into the gap, he braced his feet against the wall and gave a mighty heave. Zed, George, and Phoebe yanked hard at the wooden cross beams, but the rack remained defiant. After several more attempts Dwain took a break, then changing the position of leverage pushed his whole body weight onto the wrench. Suddenly there was a loud splintering noise, but after looking, all he had achieved was to crack the wooden upright.

Sweating, he leant against the rack. 'Those bolts are solid in that wall.'

George asked, 'Why don't we use the club hammer to smash up the brickwork around the bolts, that should loosen them?'

Phoebe was still concerned about the damage. With a rare flash of irritation at his sister he shouted. 'Oh, do shut up Pheeb, whatever we do will cause some damage.'

Dwain picked up the club hammer. 'It's worth a try.'

Taking aim, he brought it down hard. Again and again he pummelled the flaky surface, beads of sweat wetting his face. The dull sound of the prolonged thuds reverberated off the walls of the empty cavern.

Shards of brickwork and dust flew wildly from the site as he continued to pound it. Watching in awe of his strength and determination Phoebe called, 'Mind your eyes.'

When he eventually stopped, a long jagged crack had appeared alongside the bolt. He called the others over.

'Grab hold of the rack and shake it as hard as you can.'

As they did, the crack widened then two supporting bricks crumbled and fell to the floor. George yelled with excitement.

'Yeah man! We've done it!'

For the next hour Dwain ruthlessly attacked the brickwork, creating a crack or hole around the three remaining bolts, then throwing the hammer to the floor he stood back to study his destructive handywork. The others laughed at his appearance. His black hair and face were white with dust. With her sleeve Phoebe wiped the grime from his cheek, then kissed him.

'You're amazing.'

He smiled. 'I know.'

George shook his head. 'Oh, my days, that's pathetic.'

Zed asked. 'Do you think it will move now?'

Dwain nodded confidently. 'Yeah, I reckon so.'

Positioning themselves evenly around the wine rack they took hold.

Dwain shouted, 'Now when I say, rock it back and forth as hard as you can.' He took a deep breath.

'Ready! Steady !Go!'

They shook and rocked the wooden structure until their arms ached. Above their panting was a fracturing sound as the corner joints in the wood dislocated from their sockets.

'Keep going,' Dwain shouted, sensing victory. Then like an ancient tree felled by a strong gale, the whole structure lurched, tore away from its anchorage and toppled over. George and Zed who had been at the front had to leap aside as it crashed defeated to the floor. They all cheered. Triumphantly, George climbed on top of the frame as if they had slain a giant. Phoebe turned to look at the wall.

'Oh my God.'

A hole, one meter in length, had opened up; the collapsed bricks lying in a heap on the floor. As the dust settled, they found themselves staring, not as expected on to a flat surface on which the wall had been built, but a dark hollow.

# CHAPTER TWENTY THREE

## Discovery

George leaned in and waved his hand about in the darkness. It's quite deep, I can't feel anything.' Phoebe said she would fetch a torch from the kitchen. Zed thought it might have been a storeroom.

Dwain added. 'Yeah, but why brick it up?'
Zed shrugged. 'Probably didn't use it any longer.'
George asked, 'And why was that the only wine rack left down here?'

Phoebe stepped lightly down the stairs holding a large torch. She handed it to Dwain. 'Here, you look.'
George laughed. 'Scaredy cat.'

Turning it on, Dwain aimed the narrow beam into the dark hole. A large spider, startled by the intrusion of the light, scampered quickly across its wispy web. Small droplets of moisture clung effortlessly to the low uneven roof, some plopping rhythmically into puddles on the floor. Scanning the torch from left to right, he could now make out the dimensions of the hidden space. He called to the other three who were standing apprehensively behind him. 'You're right Zed, it looks like a small room.'

George asked, 'Is there anything in it?'

Dwain shook his head. 'Not that I can see, but it smells rank.'

He pushed his upper body further into the gap, so he could illuminate the furthest part. At first unsure if his eyes were playing tricks, he again trained the beam on a shadowy shape leaning at an angle against the wall. Hesitantly, he said, 'I think there's something in here.'
Phoebe asked anxiously. 'What is it?'

'I can't make it out,' replied Dwain.

George said, 'Probably a pile of junk, like the rest of the stuff that was down here.'

Dwain called Zed to take the torch whilst he climbed in.

Phoebe shrieked. 'Don't go in there!'

Despairing of his twin sister's dramatics, George laughingly said, 'There's no monster living in there.'

Zed chuckled. 'It would soon spit him out if there were.'

As Dwain hoisted himself onto the broken wall, three more bricks clattered to the floor as the now sandy mortar gave way under his weight. Slipping, he nearly fell sideways into the cavity. Phoebe gasped. Regaining his balance Dwain swung his legs across, landing onto the floor below. Zed passed the torch through the hole. He was now close to the object. His feet leaving a trail of prints in the generations of layered dust. What appeared to be an old rug covered the discarded heap. He poked it with the torch, then just like burnt newspaper it disintegrated into a musky smelling cloud.

'You alright in there?' Zed called. There was no reply.

Dwain stood riveted to the spot. A skeleton, the hollowed eye sockets staring blindly back at him. It's discoloured protruding teeth fixed in a creepy grin. Small tufts of hair clung to the rounded bald skull. Bereft of skin and muscle the hands, one outstretched, the other clenched in a fist, lay each side of the bony structure like crab claws.

Zed called again. This time Dwain found a voice, albeit dry and strangulated.

'I'm coming.' Focusing the torch beam on the hauntingly deceased form, he slowly retreated backwards towards the hole in the wall. Phoebe registered the shock on his face

'What is it? What's the matter?'

Dwain breathed in heavily before answering. 'You need to phone your parents; there's a body in there.'

George laughed. 'Yeah, ok dude! Whatever!'

Dwain shouted at him. 'Look for yourself if you don't believe me. I'm out of 'ere.'

Zed, who knew Dwain better than most, could see this was no joke. Staring into the black ghostly void, he was frozen to the spot watching Dwain's panicked scramble to get through the hole in the wall, half expecting a skeletal arm to appear and pull his friend back in. Suddenly a firm grip on Zed's arm broke the hypnotic spell, as George roughly tugged him away. 'Time to go dude.'

Phoebe had become hysterical and ran screaming towards the stairs. Dwain, dust falling from his clothes, followed hot on their heels, slamming the door of the cellar shut behind him.

They all heard the screech of tyres on the gravel drive outside. Milo and Morgan ran barking to the front door to greet their mistress. Entering the kitchen Lady Barrington Gore was not amused. She stared angrily at the four youngsters sitting at the table.

'If this is some kind of prank!' Though she could see by their grave, shocked expressions that it wasn't. Phoebe, whose hysterics hadn't abated, ran sobbing into her mother's arms.

'Mummy it's horrible. Who is it? You have to phone the police right away.' She stroked her daughter's hair, attempting to calm her down.

Minutes later an equally ruffled Sir Roland arrived home. Highly miffed at being disturbed on the golf course, his language to them was less polite. He did though listen calmly as they recounted the morning's events in the cellar, then concluded, 'Before we do anything, show me where it is.'

Phoebe and George exchanged concerned looks at having to go back down there. Dwain stood up. 'I'll show you.'

Within an hour of Sir Roland's phone call, the scene at Manor House resembled the set of a television police drama. Forensic and scene of crime officers wearing white suits and gloves shuffled quietly and efficiently to and from the underground tomb. Uniformed officers stood outside, others by the gate. Before the police arrived, Zed had phoned Peggy at the cottage to recount the morning's events and the subsequent dark discovery. She had listened to him in horrified disbelief. Concerned about them, particularly Dwain, she suggested ringing Tim and driving straight over. Knowing Tim's antipathy to the Barrington Gores, Zed laughed.

'I don't think he will be too happy about that Peg.'

She snorted. 'That's too bad love, he'll have to swallow his pride.'

Reassuring her that they were both fine, he promised to ring when they could leave to come back.

In the library on the ground floor, two detectives copied down statements from the four youngsters, patiently challenging any inconsistencies in their related accounts. Across the room at another table, a Detective Chief Inspector Sidney Cross was talking to Sir Roland and Lady Barrington Gore. Given the presumed age of the skeleton in the cellar, he wanted information about previous occupiers. Sir Roland explained that the Manor House had been in his family for generations.

The library door opened and one of the forensic officers beckoned to DCI Cross.

He spoke to him briefly, then handed over a clear plastic evidence bag. Returning to the table, the detective laid it down in front of Sir Roland and Lady Barrington Gore.

'This item was clasped in one of the victim's hands. Do you recognise it?'

Enclosed was a small round enamelled badge with the King's Crown at the top; in the centre a golden coloured wheatsheaf against a dark green background.

'May I?' asked Lady Barrington Gore, putting on her glasses. The officer nodded. Picking up the evidence bag she studied the lettering around the edges of the badge.

She read aloud, 'Woman's Land Army.'

Then as realisation dawned upon her, she gasped, and turned to face Sir Roland.

'The article in the Echo. You remember the girl who went missing during the war.'

Confused, the officer asked, 'Sorry what article is this?'

Sir Roland quickly stood up. 'Good grief, I forgot all about that. It's still in my study upstairs. I'll fetch it.'

Lady Barrington Gore was gripped with despair at the notion. 'So that poor thing could have been here all that time, right under our noses?'

The Chief Inspector shrugged. 'Quite possibly,' he sighed. 'The question now though is, was she murdered, and by whom? Who hid the body there, and was it the same person?'

Breathlessly, Sir Roland arrived back in the room clutching the copy of the Melbury Echo. He laid it on the table and pointed to the header on the article by the journalist Adi Adekola.

## EXCLUSIVE
### Local Man's Theory on Missing Land Army Girl, Daisy Kearns

The officer picked it up and studiously read through the text, then without comment took an evidence bag from his pocket and dropped it inside. Sir Roland asked, 'Do you think.............?'

The Chief Inspector interrupted him. 'We'll know more when we have the pathology report.'
It was early evening when a private ambulance arrived to remove the remains. As Sir Roland and Lady Barrington Gore watched the gurney being wheeled across the spacious entrance hall, her composure collapsed like a burst dam, and she sobbed freely.

Tim had earlier collected Zed and Dwain and taken them back to the cottage. That night George slept in Phoebe's room. Sir Roland and Lady Barrington Gore didn't sleep at all.

The following day, lounging in the small teashop fronting Tiddledurn High Street, Rocket Ron waited in anticipation for the arrival of Heather Reynolds. Following the telephone discussion earlier in the week, he had formed a mental picture of the woman he was about to meet. Scanning passing pedestrians, he watched for a stranger who matched his perceived description. His assumptions though proved wildly inaccurate as he was approached by a trim, well dressed lady with neat greying hair.

'Mr Hughes I assume.' She held out a gloved hand.

He stood. 'Call me Ron, please.'

'It's so nice to meet you in person Ron.' He detected a hint of scent, but it wasn't Mugler Angel.

'What a charming village,' she observed hanging her blue jacket on the chair. 'I've often wondered what Tiddledurn looked like.' This comment struck him as odd, but he didn't ask why.

She ordered an Earl Grey tea with a twist of lemon. He stuck to the builder's version, albeit served in a decorative bone china cup. Slowly stirring in one brown sugar lump she said, 'When I heard about your article in the Echo and you're interest in the case, I felt compelled to put the record straight about Albert Cooke. It's been too long.' She took a sip of tea. 'You are no doubt wondering who I am?' Ron nodded attentively. She continued. 'Albert and Mary Cook had a daughter called Alice.' She paused. 'She was my mother.'

Ron's eyes widened. 'But I thought............'

She smiled. 'Not that child, sadly he was adopted. I presume you are acquainted with the story about that.'

Ron said he was.

'Very well, then you will also know that my grandfather owned a garage here in Tiddledurn.' She paused and looked at the modern petrol station across the road. 'That very one I believe.'

She took another sip of tea. 'In 1938, my grandparents had taken out a considerable bank loan on the garage. Then the war came, and the business crashed. There was little petrol to be had and subsequently far fewer vehicles on the road. They struggled to keep it going, but it was becoming more difficult to make the monthly loan repayments and pay the rent for their house. The future was looking very bleak for them and my mother. So, rightly or wrongly they devised a plan of action. My grandfather would fake his disappearance, giving the impression that he had somehow died, though a body would never be found. Then after a time my grandmother would receive the small life insurance. In the meantime, she would sell the garage and pay off the depts.

Astonished, Ron asked. 'But where did they go afterwards? 'My grandmother's sister lived in Coventry. Her husband was away fighting in the war, so they moved in with her. My grandfather, Albert, who had been lying low followed them sometime later. She chuckled. 'My mother said they all laughed when he had turned up. He looked like an unwashed vagrant with long hair and a beard. The insurance money turned out to be a lifesaver, as it was ages before he found another job. Eventually though he was offered a mechanic's position at a garage in Brinklow near Coventry. They found a small cottage to rent in the village and stayed there until the end of their days.'

Ron shook his head. 'Wow, that's some story. So, there was nothing sinister in his disappearance then?'

Smiling, she shook her head. 'I'm afraid not Ron. Sorry to disappoint all the conspiracy theories. Now you see why I wanted to talk to you and not the journalist. My family would obviously not want this appearing in the local paper.'

She paused to check her emotions. 'Sadly my mother, Alice, was dying of cancer when she revealed all this to me, also that I have an older half brother living somewhere.'

Ron ordered two more teas then asked, 'Will you try to trace your brother?'

She shrugged. 'It would be nice to locate him, but where would one start, it's been such a long time. Maybe if I had known about his existence sooner?'

'And what about you, Heather? Where do you hale from?' She chuckled. 'Oh, I'm a Midlands girl through and through. Alice married my father, an engineer at the Hillman car plant in Coventry in 1947, she was twenty six, I was born a year later.'

They exchanged life stories for another hour before leaving the tea shop. For a moment she stood on the pavement looking across at her grandfather's old garage, then turning to Ron she said,

'You forget the life you had before.....after a while.'

Ron watched as this elegant messenger from the past walked off towards the car park. As he turned to go in the opposite direction, there was a call on his mobile, that irritating 'Nokia' tone which he kept meaning to change. It was Peggy to tell him about the discovery of the body at the Manor House.

He walked a few paces along the street then sat on a bench opposite an old water trough, now filled with spring flowers. He smiled and closed his eyes. 'I'll bet a pound to a penny it's you Daisy Kearns.' For the first time in days, the dullness in his mind had cleared.

# CHAPTER TWENTY FOUR

## Black Sheep

For Zed and Dwain it was a serene contrast to the drama of the previous day at the Manor House. Warm soft breezes whispered soothingly from the adjoining fields. At the edges, pink and yellow wildflowers grew where nature's breath had lain the seeds. Populated by aloof mute swans, chattering ducks and darting moorhens, the narrow channel drifted lazily past lightly wooded fields and meadows.

They ceased paddling the double canoe named Black Jack, after the notorious highwayman, and glided silently across the murky surface of the canal. They had reached Harry Martin's marina where Tim and Peggy would be taking over the management following Harry's disabling heart attack. Looking through the narrow entrance they could still see the burnt out hull of the narrowboat hugging the fire-blackened pontoon. Zed said, 'I can't believe all this has happened to us in such a short time. Dwain made a backward flip on the paddle to turn the canoe around in the direction of the cottage. He laughed. 'And it's supposed to be quieter down here than in London.'

As they approached the bridge hole where the eighteenth century stonework spanned the meandering thread; a woman's voice, clear and sharp in volume. Startled, both boys turned, expecting to see someone calling to them.

Thick rich greens of blackthorn and elder bush. Water reed and white-flowering meadow sweet at the verges. The scampering of a water vole and hovering midnight blue dragonfly. Virgin air as clear as glass, but no human form to be seen anywhere.

Dwain said, 'That's weird man, I could swear I heard a woman's voice.'

Zed agreed. 'Me too.'
Above the bridge an elderly man walking a dog waved to them. Dwain called to him.

'Have you seen a woman?'
Laughing, he shook his head. 'I should be so lucky lad.'

Sammy and Sheena, Tim's two adopted swans were gliding lazily about the canal when the boys arrived back at the lock. Lifting Black Jack from the water they carried it to the storage rack at the rear of the cottage. In the kitchen Peggy and Gran were busy serving Sunday lunch, the aroma of roast pork permeated the air, tempting the boy's hungry appetites. Tim poked his head through the open window. 'Come on you two, foods on the table. Time and tide.' 'Wait for no one.' chorused Zed and Dwain.


All was not so peaceful at the home of the Barrington Gores two weeks later, when Detective Chief Inspector Sidney Cross and his sidekick Sergeant Gould made their final visit to the Manor House. They brought with them the pathologist's report which had determined that the remains were those of a young woman. Tests on the bone density indicated that death had occurred between seventy and eighty years ago.

Sir Roland asked, 'But do we know if she was murdered?'
The DCI's answer was non-committal. 'The condition of the body makes that almost impossible to establish.' Then with a wry smile, he stated sardonically,

'However, one has to ask why anyone would voluntarily choose to die bricked up behind a wall.' Taking the Melbury Echo article from his pocket he laid it on the table.

'It would appear this chap Ron Hughes was onto something. After cutting through much historic red tape the Ministry of Defence have confirmed to us that a special agent was installed here in March 1942 under the codename Operation Green Fields.'

As they settled themselves in the library, Sir Roland asked, 'And was that person......?'

The sergeant cut in. 'Yes. Daisy Kearns. But unfortunately, without anything to match DNA against we can't say for certain if the body in your cellar was her. As such we are treating the death as suspicious, with our main suspects being the occupiers of the house at the time.'

Lady Barrington Gore protested loudly. 'Why on earth would Wilf and Edgar be involved in anything like this? It doesn't make any sense.'

The Chief Inspector nodded thoughtfully 'Maybe not both of them.' Producing another document, he laid it on the table alongside the Melbury Echo article. 'We obtained this from Somerset House in London. It is a copy of Edgar Barrrington Gores death certificate issued on the 21st May 1972.'

Sir Roland said, 'Yes, he's buried in the family crypt at St Mark's churchyard.'

The DCI continued. 'Exactly. But no such certification of Wilf's death could be found, nor I believe does he reside at St Mark's alongside his brother.'

Anticipating his wife's searching question, Sir Roland shrugged. 'Apart from my father, how would I know who is in there?'

She stood up shaking her head. 'I'll go to the kitchen and make some tea.'

Phoebe and George were sitting in the kitchen, their homework spread out across the table.

'Have the police gone Ma?' George asked his mother.

'No. More questions I'm afraid.'

Phoebe, who was generally more studious than her brother, sat pawing apathetically through her English text book. Suddenly she yelled. 'I hate it, I can't stand being here.'

With a hint of irritation her mother said, 'Phoebe, be sensible. What else can we do, we can't just up and move out.'

Phoebe retorted defiantly. 'Why not? We could go and stay with Gran in Sidmouth.'

George replied, 'I'm not going down to that boring place, it's full of old wrinklies.'

Lady Barrington Gore replied sharply. 'It's out of the question, anyway, you both have to go to school.'

Phoebe threw her pen down on the table. 'I don't know how you can sleep at nights knowing there was a body in the cellar.'

George chuckled. 'My mates at school thought it was cool.'

Exasperated, Phoebe jumped up and stormed from the kitchen. Lady Barrington Gore gave her son a withering look. 'Do you have to wind her up?'

He shrugged innocently. 'What?'

His mother shook her head in despair and headed for the library.

DCI Cross pushed aside the documents as Lady Barrington Gore placed the tea tray on the table.

'My children are chalk and cheese,' she said. 'One is on the verge of a nervous breakdown, the other thinks its 'cool.'

Sir Roland laughed. 'No guessing which is which.'

The sergeant took a digestive biscuit from the plate and dunked it in his tea. Aware of his superior's disapproving look, Sir Roland laughed. 'Don't worry we do it all the time.'

DCI Cross stirred three spoons of sugar into his tea. 'Now where were we? Ah, yes. Wilf flew to Germany in March 1939. We know this, as police at the time arrested the pilot on his return on suspicion of smuggling.'

Sergeant Gould added. 'We believe he may have stayed with your relatives, the Westerhugans, in Munich.'

Sensing where this may be going Sir Roland said, 'But they were a respected family.'

The DCI nodded. 'Quite so.' He pushed the tea tray aside and laid down two printed copies of emails sent from the 'Bundespolizei' in Berlin. 'It seems the Nazi's were, if nothing else, highly efficient at keeping records, many of which still exist. The Westerhugans, being an old German aristocrat family, were not supporters of Hitler's regime. However, their eldest son Klaus, Wilf's cousin, was. He joined the SS, serving with the......' He pointed to the email, 'I won't try to pronounce it. Sicherheitsdienst des Reichsfuhrers . They were the intelligence agency of the Nazi party, and Klaus Westerhugan's section were responsible for monitoring the activities of the French Resistance, then relaying this information to Gestapo Headquarters in Paris.'

Sir Roland asked, 'This is all very interesting, but I still don't see how Wilf is linked to this.'
The sergeant dunked another biscuit.

'We have trawled through local police records of the time. The landlord of the Red Lion pub in Tiddledurn reported that a local man had identified Wilf entering this house in a car on the night of 21st September 1942.'

'So, he did come back from Germany then?' asked Lady Barrington Gore.
The sergeant nodded. 'If this chap's report is credible, yes.'

DCI Sidney Cross started to gather up the documents on the table. 'So, with a big dollop of supposition, for we'll never be able to prove it conclusively, we believe that Wilf was recruited by Klaus to intercept classified information being received at Ivy House.'

The sergeant added. 'And when Daisy Kearns unearthed him, he murdered her before she could reveal his identity.'

Sir Roland stood up and walked across to the window. 'This is dreadful, dreadful. I just cannot believe it; a British traitor in our family.'

At first Lady Barrington Gore was too shell shocked to say anything. Then she asked, 'Do you know what happened to him after the war?'

A satisfied smile played on Sid Cross's lips. 'Thanks to our friends in the Bundespolizei we do. He was killed in an allied air raid on Berlin in 1945.'

She shook her head in disbelief. 'Oh my God, so he went back there.'

Sergeant Gould chuckled. 'The fox always returns to its lair.'

DCI Cross stood. 'Well..... this concludes our investigation. I'll be preparing a report for the coroner. I expect you will be called as witnesses. Sir Roland, Lady Barrington Gore, thank you for your cooperation.'

As they were leaving the house, Sergeant Gould turned to the couple and said, 'Many families have a black sheep.'

Zed, Dwain, George, and Phoebe were sitting on the mound enjoying their lunchtime break. White shirted youngsters dotted the surrounding Melbury Comprehensive school fields like grazing sheep. Despite their parents attempts to keep the family's dirty washing in the machine Phoebe and George, unable to keep secrets, were eager to reveal the latest 'body in the cellar' revelations to their friends. Phoebe had become less neurotic since her father had said he would seal up the cellar. George though, always ready to tease his twin sister, had pointed out that it would make no difference as ghosts could pass through walls. Dwain had his arm around Phoebe. Zed and George sat close to each other but were conscious of not drawing peer group attention to their relationship.

Overhead a plane, the sun glinting off its fuselage, ploughed a chalky furrow across the blue cloudless expanse. It reminded Zed and Dwain of their past lives in South London. From the balcony of the flats they would watch the planes skimming overhead as they approached City airport, dreaming that they, one day, might be aboard.

Now approaching sixteen and on the cusp of adulthood, where would the flight of destiny carry them and their friends to in the future.

# PREVIOUS BOOKS BY THE AUTHOR

## The Stowaway Series

The Stowaway
The Golden Windlass
The Strangers
The Breaking Point

## Other titles

One Paddle Short of a Lock
Pecked Bread and Fallen Leaves.  A collection of poetry